Out
Past
the Wires

Rod Picott

MEZCALITA
PRESS

Mezcalita Press, LLC
Norman, Oklahoma

MEZCALITA PRESS, LLC
Norman, Oklahoma

Out
Past
the Wires

Short Stories
by

Rod Picott

MEZCALITA
PRESS

Table of Contents

Acknowledgements

Thanks to:
Nathan Brown
Ashley Brown
Stacie Huckeba
Jennie Carlsten
Tasha Thomas
Lloyd Picott
Lois Picott
Ron Rash
Brian Koppelman
Nicholson Baker
Donald Ray Pollock
Andre Dubus lll
Tamara Saviano

Out

Past

the Wires

Coal

Ben Carmon's hands were stained a permanent black. Daily, at the utility sink in the entryway to his home, he scrubbed them with harsh Lava soap, but the dark lines of his palms' geography remained. Ben had worked the coal mines along the Pittsburgh seam for twenty years. Early on, he worked close to his home in Putnam County. As the years went by and the mines moved west, he was forced to drive further each morning in his Ford F-150 pickup. By the late 90's, Ben was driving ninety minutes each way to work. Each morning, he rose quietly at five AM so as not to disturb his sleeping wife Nellie, a teacher at the local elementary school. He dressed himself for work in the hallway after softly shutting their bedroom door. His dirty boots waited in the mud room.

Ben found his way to the kitchen, poured strong black coffee into a Thermos for the long drive, grabbed his lunch pail from the ancient Frigidaire and walked out into the chilly black morning. He started the old Ford. The starter was failing, so he had to jab the metal housing with a long pole he kept in the bed of his truck. Money was tight now and he could not afford a new starter just yet, though he was squirreling a few dollars away to get one from the You-Pull-It junkyard. The starter was getting worse, though, and on this morning, Ben had to stab several times with the pole.

On his drive to work, Ben listened to the local AM radio station to hear the scores of the local football teams and the day's news. The signal lasted until Perryville, where he switched to an FM country music station. In Williamson County, the signal faded again and he tuned the dial to a classic rock radio station until he arrived at the mine. The sound of Bad Company filled the cab as the old truck pulled to a dusty halt in the parking area.

"Mornin' Ben," Carl, the pit boss, said.

"Yes it is," said Ben.

"Not sure if the word got around, but we're losing another twenty or so."

"But we just got to the meat of the seam, Carl."

"I know, but these new shuttle cars are so much faster with the longwallers than those old shuttle cars. We can't keep men on when we don't need 'em."

"Damn. Have they made the cuts yet?"

"Not yet. I'll put in a word for you. You've always been good here."

"I appreciate it."

Ben pulled a cigarette from a pack of Basic menthols and lit it. Most days, he arrived a few minutes early so he could enjoy a smoke before starting the long dark walk down into the hole. Today, he found he didn't enjoy the cigarette as he pulled hard on it. There was a nervous feeling in his gut. He leaned on the fender of the Ford and watched Carl walk back to the portable metal building that served as the office. Ben locked the doors of the Ford and walked to the hole and went down in. The familiar smell comforted him and the cool darkness eased the tension wringing his body.

At the house, Nellie woke lying wide across the bed. She lay a few minutes, staring at the ceiling, listening to the birds outside the window, then got up, put on her robe and went to wake the children. Ben Jr. and Tina, two years apart at twelve and ten, were good kids who did moderately well in school without excelling at anything in particular. Ben Jr. played peewee football, loved sports, was small for his age but did well regardless. Tina was a quiet bookish sort and read constantly. In the room they still shared, Nellie gently shook the kids awake, then went to the kitchen to make breakfast. She scrambled eggs and made toast while sipping from the coffee Ben had left warming in the pot for her. As the kids ate, she looked over bills, wrote out a few checks, and looked at the latest bank statement. The mortgage would be late again, but so far they were staying afloat. Things had changed from years before when Ben had been in the Union. The wages were better then; there had been health insurance.

It took Ben nearly an hour to reach the wall they were working deep underground. He checked the hydraulics of the huge continuous mining machine and inspected its toothed drum. He walked around the machine, inspecting the moving joints, making sure they were properly greased. He put his ear protection on and started the beast to its chewing. Black soot immediately filled the air in the deep room, and he pulled his breathing mask over his face. The smells of menthol cigarette and coal dust mixed in his nose. For several hours, he operated the machine by remote control as it tore away several tons of coal from the vein. At eleven, he handed the remote over to another man. They nodded at each other in the noise, and Ben walked out of the depth to his truck and lunch pail. When he opened his pail, he saw sitting at the top a note that said "Love

You!", a heart shape drawn around the words. Ben ate his sandwich and sipped his lukewarm coffee in the driver's seat. Both truck doors were open to let a small acrid breeze float through the cabin. Dust covered every inch of the truck's interior save for the steering wheel and bench seat. A faint "Ben" was traced onto the dashboard in a child's stiff penmanship. A man approached the truck, carrying the same lunch pail and sat himself into the passenger's side.

"You hear about it?" asked the man.

"Yeah, I heard," said Ben.

"What you think?"

"I suspect they're buying a longwaller."

"You think?"

"I do. If they are, it means a lot more than twenty of us are gone."

"You're right about that."

"They're saying twenty now, but it'll be more than twice that. That machine can pull a hundred tons a day."

"Fuckin' A."

"What are we gonna do?"

"I don't know. Carl was trying to be cool about it, but I got a bad feeling."

"Carl ain't had to wash his hands in twenty-five years."

"He's okay. What the hell is he supposed to do about it? It's the guys wearing ties that's making this happen."

"Well, fuck," said the man, then bit his sandwich.

"I'd say that's about right," said Ben, pulling a cigarette from the pack lying between them. He lit the cigarette and pulled deeply from it.

Ben finished his smoke, the man finished his sandwich and they walked back and down into the hole.

At the elementary school, Nellie finished grading the day's papers, neatened her desk and walked to her car. In the parking lot, she saw June Martin, another teacher, leaving for the day.

"Hi, June."

"Hi, Nellie. What do you think about this?"

"About what?"

"The mine. I hear they're switching to a longwall machine."

"What do you mean?"

"It's a bigger machine. There are going to be lay-offs."

"I haven't heard about it."

"Eddie told me last night. He saw the paperwork at the office."

"How many?"

"I don't know. Eddie said maybe as many as fifty."

"Oh, god, I hope not."

"It's not good."

"Are you sure?"

"Yes. Eddie saw the paperwork for it."

"How soon?"

"Could be soon, in a few weeks maybe."

"If you hear any more, let me know?"

"Sure, Nellie. Fingers crossed for Eddie and Ben…"

When Ben returned home he stood at the utility sink scrubbing hard at the black lines on his red calloused hands. He went into the kitchen. The two children sat at the table doing homework. Nellie was at the stove cooking. Ben sat himself at the table and was quiet.

"Jane told me something today, Ben."

"Yeah, I know. Not now, okay?"

"Okay."

Ben watched his son checking boxes on a multiple-choice paper. He looked at his son's small frame and wondered when puberty would kick in, and if his son would catch up in size. He'd hoped that with his son's natural ability at sports, there might be scholarship opportunities in the future. Looking at the boy now, he worried; a dark vague unknown.

"Clear the table, you two. Dinner is ready," Nellie said.

The two children picked up their papers and scurried off to their rooms. Nellie set the table.

"I just don't want them to worry," Ben whispered.

"I know."

"It's been hard enough lately."

"Is it true? June said Eddie saw the paperwork."

"Yeah. I talked to Carl today. He said he'd put in a word for me, but I have a bad feeling. I've been doing room and pillar for so long, and they have other guys who've been on a longwaller before. I don't know it. No one else is hiring. That Ford isn't going to last much longer with this drive."

"What would we do?"

"I don't know."

The two children returned to the table. Nellie served dinner and they ate. After the table was cleared, the children watched the television while Nellie made Ben's lunch for the following day. Ben

prepared the coffee machine and set the timer to
4:30. After the children went to bed, Ben and Nellie
lay side by side on their own bed. Ben reached out
his hand and held hers tightly.

"It'll be okay, Nell. We'll figure something out.
We've always figured something out."

"I know. But it gets harder and harder. There's
nothing left. The mortgage is late again."

They lay quiet, side by side for a long time –
each in their own ponderings. Outside the window,
the last of the day's birds sang in the distance. Nellie
moved to reach for Ben, but he stopped her hand.

"I can't right now, Nell."

"Okay."

The next morning Ben again had to crack at the
starter several times with the pole. At last the starter
caught the flywheel and the engine turned over.
When he arrived at the mine, he saw it. The
monstrous machine sat bright garish yellow in the
morning sun. He saw Carl stepping into the office
and followed him. Ben knocked at the door.

"Yeah?"

"Hey, Carl, can I step in for a sec?"

"Yup."

Ben walked into the office and closed the door
gently.

"So, already?"

"Yeah. It's pretty, ain't it?"

"You got names yet?"

"At the end of the day."

"So do I need to worry?"

"You've always been great here, Ben."

"Yeah, but do I need to worry?"

"C'mon, Ben, you know I can't say anything. It's policy. I gotta wait until the end of the day." He did not look up from the papers in front of him.

"Damn, Carl."

"I know, Ben. I know."

At lunch Ben was joined again in his Ford.

"This is bad," said the man as he bit into his sandwich.

"Yeah, this is bad," Ben said, his lunch box unopened. Several cigarette butts littered the ground outside the driver's side of the truck and another glowed between his fingers as he filled his lungs.

At the end of the day, the men gathered outside the portable metal office building as Carl nervously called names and handed out slips. An occasional curse was hurled.

"Ben Carmon," Carl said without looking up from the slips in his hand. Ben walked forward. He looked directly at Carl, but Carl did not look up. Ben grabbed the slip from his hand. He walked to the Ford, got in, rolled the window down, lit a cigarette and sat silent watching the other, mostly older, men take their slips. Slowly, the parking area emptied. Ben sat smoking. Eventually Carl came out of the office, walked quickly to his shining new truck, then drove away. Ben sat alone in the lot.

He smoked another cigarette, then turned the key in the ignition. The engine turned over on the first try. Ben put the truck into gear and started to pull away. As he neared the exit, he saw the massive yellow machine gleaming in the low sun. He stopped the truck, then cut the engine. He sat for a moment staring at the machine. Ben got out of the cab and opened the rusted toolbox in the bed of his truck. He pulled out a pair of large metal snips, walked to the longwaller and started cutting. He cut hydraulic hoses. He cut wiring. He continued to cut everything the snips would bite into. Oil leaked freely from the machine onto the ground. A huge puddle of golden unspoiled oil pooled like blood in some strange abattoir. He walked back to his Ford, got in, and turned the key, but the engine didn't turn. Ben grabbed the pole and knocked at the starter housing. The engine did not turn over. He tried again and still the flywheel would not catch the motor. Again and he again, he knocked at the starter, but the engine would not catch. He sat in the truck smoking, tried again, but the truck would not start. Come morning, Ben sat in his dusty truck, smoking his last cigarette beside the felled beast.

A Better Man

Bender remembered the child in all his pink rawness. The boy's tiny fists were curling and uncurling. His toes stretching for footing they could not find in the sanitized air of the hospital room. The baby's red pug-face was like an old fighter sucking for air he could not pull in. His first round was his last, and then the tiny casket. Bender had not liked the surprise of the death gown. His boy in a dress felt wrong. But he had no religion and Charlene was Catholic and so that was how it was done. The doctors had no answers. His heavy fists could find no satisfaction in why the thing had happened. Then he had lost Charlene as well. He watched her slowly recede from his grasp. First there was the crushing weight of the six-pound loss, then the long slow breach and eventual break between her heart and his. It was so slow he couldn't see it happening – like the movement of the earth's plates, and just as unstoppable.

Bender slid his sweating beer bottle along the bar top, watching the centipede markings form and reform as if a living thing. He peeled the label off the bottle gingerly with his thick fingers, pulling slowly as it came off in one complete wet piece. Above the bar, the Boston Celtics were beating the New York Knicks on the television. A ticker of other games' scores scrolled endlessly from left to right. He laid the label flat on the bar in line with the five others and pressed the air out from underneath it with his big thumbs so that it was stuck to the bar like a shiny sticker. He finished the bottle in one long chug and motioned to the bartender for another.

"Maybe you should slow down, Ben."

"This is slow."

The bartender didn't argue and slid another cold beer to him. Bender sat on the stool leaning over the bar, his massive shoulders sloped and his head hung down staring at the arrangement of labels – his own personal flags. Allegiance to the country of Budweiser. Since losing Charlene, Bender had taken up a nightly residency at the Cartier Club. He often drank himself into a stupor and many mornings he had no recollection of getting home. The bar was walking distance to his small spartan apartment.

At the age of forty-eight, every single thing in Bender's entire world didn't fill a seven hundred square-foot apartment. Once his life had consisted of Charlene, their shared hopes of a family, and dreams new and old to unfold with each other. Now his life's yield was comprised of a toaster oven; a single drawer of clothes; a box of photographs; a black and white television; and a pair of boxing gloves, a souvenir of his younger self that hung from a rusted hook on the back of his bathroom door. It felt to him that he'd not come out on the better end of the trade from his past life to his current.

"Hit me," said Bender

"Oh, Ben, come on now. Slow down."

"Hit me."

"You know that's not even an American beer, don't you?" someone said.

"What?"

"That's not an American beer. Some big European country owns it."

Bender looked at the bartender incredulously. The bartender shrugged.

"I just get it from the distributor. I don't give a shit who owns it until someone buys it from me. As far as I'm concerned, if it's in my bar – I own it until you buy it," said the bartender.

"I'm talking about the company," the man said.

Bender swung his hulk toward the man.

"Stop talking."

"I'm just saying everybody thinks…" the stranger trailed off as Bender stared directly into his eyes. The man took his beer and went to sit near the pool table where two young men were playing eight ball. A stacked pile of quarters claimed the table for them.

Back in his apartment, Bender lay on his Goodwill bed staring at the ceiling light. Two bare forty-watt bulbs glowed. On the floor beside his bed, a beer was sweating through its label. The black and white television set crackled the end of the Celtics game. The picture blinked every few seconds. An ornament of tinfoil was arranged on each of the rabbit ear antennae. Bender finished the beer, then reached up for the light switch. The room went dark except for the dancing bluish light of the flickering television set, and Bender closed his eyes waiting for sleep to find him. Deep in the night, the sound of the television woke him; he shut it off and stood staring out the bedroom window. The streetlight lit the sidewalk below him. A cat slinked out from under a parked car and ran panicked across the street from some unseen terror. Without warning, tears filled his eyes and he found himself weeping deeply at a loss that had no name. Hope, he thought to himself when he recovered, was what made you weak. He'd had hope before, known it, named it, felt it in his bones. He wished he'd never known this thing that had been taken from him.

He went back to bed and sleep found him again. He dreamed he was boxing. He felt the hard leather at the stitching of the other man's glove cut his face and open a huge gash above his eye. He was on the ropes. The other fighter was much faster. He pulled his gloves up to his face and pulled his elbows together, but the man's punches were finding their way through. The cut opened wider. Blood ran into his eyes and he could not see. Over and over, punches landed while his dream self was slow, almost immobile, and unable to defend. Then he discovered that the pain felt good to him. Body, body, head. The punches came like a vicious rain and the pain in his ribs, kidneys, liver, and swollen face were a mysterious consecration he gave himself over to.

When he woke, Bender felt lighter for a short time. He made coffee, dressed for work, and went down the staircase to his 1975 Datsun B-210. Getting into the car, he felt the heaviness come back in a wave. At six foot two and two hundred twenty pounds, Bender looked ridiculous in the tiny car. Charlene had wanted the Firebird and in his grief he'd not had the strength to fight over it. Bender had let her have it all – and even in the losses of things, he felt a small kind of atonement. He parked the car outside the manufactured-home factory, punched his card, and started in.

Bender had worked construction for most of his adult life and had done well at times. He knew most of the trades and had always been a quick learner. After losing the baby and then Charlene, he had also lost the will to run his own operation. He settled into an easy by-the-hour job at the factory where he had little responsibility and did not have to bring his work home to his tiny apartment. For several months, he'd been on the roofing crew. The enormous facility was a dangerous place. Many of the men were rough and though some of them were skilled at their trades, like Bender they were men who either lacked ambition or had been taken down a notch by life and drifted into the simple nine-to-five existence. Dust floated in the sun that burned down through the skylights of the building. Pneumatic nail guns popped like firecrackers. Saws screamed at the wood they bit into. The air was filled with a cocktail of smells. Cut wood, pungent adhesives, chemical douses and the odor of hard-working men mixed together in the giant building.

Bender lifted three bundles of asphalt shingles onto his wide shoulder and climbed the ladder to the roof of the half house – split right down the middle, then assembled later onsite. He laid the bundles down, ripped open one pack, and went about laying out almost a full square. Then he went back with a nail gun and, pulling back the safety with one hand, he quickly nailed the entire row of shingles into place. Bender repeated the ritual for hours. At the end of the day, he punched his card, nodded at a few other men as he left and drove home in the tiny Datsun.

At home, Bender showered, then heated a frozen dinner and ate it while he downed two beers. He walked the three blocks to the Cartier Club and took his seat at the bar. The bartender slid him a cold bottle of Budweiser and he nodded thanks. Above the bar, the Boston Celtics were losing to the Detroit Pistons, though it was early in the game. Bender finished his beer and waved for another, which slid across the bar right into his big left palm. He nodded. The bartender walked the length of the bar and stood in front of Bender.

"How come you don't do this at home?"

"What?"

"You come in here almost every night. You sit there and drink eight or ten beers. You're not watching the game. You don't talk to nobody. You don't meet nobody. You don't play pool. You just sit there and drink. You been coming here about a year now and that's what you do. I mean, I'm happy for the business, don't get me wrong, but why not just sit at home? It's a lot cheaper to just buy a case."

"You got color television."

"That's why you come here?"

"Yeah."

"Okay. We got color television. I guess that's as good as any reason."

Back at his apartment, Bender thought about Charlene. They'd been together for five years and lived together for four when she finally got pregnant. He remembered her telling him. She'd made a big deal that she had news for him and she had taken him out to dinner – insisting that *she* was taking *him* out. He had already guessed. They'd been trying for a couple years and her excitement had been too much for her news to be anything other than what it was. He'd been excited as well. They had a great time of making plans, picking out paint for the baby's room, opening a new savings account. Bender had even stopped boxing. He was long past his prime at that point, but still enjoyed the sport and the rituals of training. He remembered feeling the enormity of the wide-open future for them all as his past life dropped away and he fell fully into his new life with Charlene and the idea of family. He had never felt as happy as when he lay in bed with her in those months, feeling her stomach, the two of them slowly becoming three.

That night, the dream came to him again. He was boxing. His limbs were stiff in his dream – as though cement coursed his veins in place of blood. Backed into the corner of the ring, the other fighter pounded away at him. He heard his own grunts with each punch he took, and the high "seeth" that came from the other man's mouthpiece. He spit his own mouthpiece out. The other fighter adjusted and threw at his jaw. A right hook connected, and he collapsed in the corner of the ring. Then he woke. Bender was sweating and the sheets were cool and wet against his skin. The television flickered in the peeling wallpaper of the room. He got out of bed, shut the television off and stood at the window again. The same cat crept nervous and low down the sidewalk, its ears pricked listening for some unheard thing. The streetlight radiated at the same height as his second floor apartment and hurt his eyes. He drained the rest of a warm beer that sat beside the bed, then lay down, fell asleep, but did not dream again.

Bender woke, made coffee, and drove to work. At the lunch break, he punched his card and walked out to the truck that arrived daily with hot coffee, soda and hot sandwiches. Standing in line to order, an argument broke out between two men in front of him.

"Back of the line, hoss," said the bigger man.

"Fuck you, I'm giving Jimmy my money so he can order for me."

"The fuck you are. Back of the line, hoss."

"What's it got to do with you? Mind your own fucking business."

"Because if we start this shit, there's gonna be one asshole out here getting orders for ten guys and we'll all be waiting just as long anyway, so get to the back of the line and order your own damn lunch like everybody else."

The other men in line turned and craned to watch the two. Some grinned, hoping it would escalate; some felt a nervous electricity run through them. Bender felt nothing, but stood listening.

"It's got nothing to do with you." But the man's voice had gone soft and everyone knew he had yielded. The men turned their attention back to the lunch truck as he took his money back from Jimmy and walked to the back of the long line.

When Bender's turn arrived, he ordered two sandwiches, two coffees and two bags of chips. He paid. As he passed, he handed half the order to the small man at the back of the line. The man took the food awkwardly – not understanding, he dropped the bag of chips, picked it up and fumbled for his money, but Bender kept walking.

"Hey!" The bigger man yelled at Bender.

Bender turned fully around, looking directly into the man's eyes with no expression. The other man held his hands out, palms up as if to ask a question for which he had no words. Bender stared down through and past him, as if his eyes were merely holes in his head that he could see clear through. The man turned back around and a small shudder went through him that he hoped no one saw.

"You don't want any part of that," said the man inside the lunch truck.

"Just give me my fucking food."

That night, as Bender sat at the bar drinking, a thing clicked and turned over in his head. He wasn't quite sure what it was, but felt a distinct change as though the air pressure in the room had plummeted suddenly. He motioned for the bartender, who instinctively pulled another beer from the cooler in front of him, but Bender waived it off.

"I'm gonna settle."

"Okay, Ben. What's up?"

"I don't know. I'm just… I don't know."

"It's Friday night…"

"I don't know."

Bender paid the bartender and tipped him a five, then walked home. He looked at the cheap alarm clock on the floor next to the bed. There were hundreds of dark round water stains in the pine floorboards near the clock. It was just past eight o'clock. He went to the bathroom and stared into the mirror. Bender stared into his reflected eyes long enough that his face became distorted to him and frightened him in a small strange way. As he was leaving the tiny bathroom with its foam green tiles, he pulled at the door. The old boxing gloves still hung from the hook where he had put them the day he'd moved in. He reached out and felt his hands along the soft beaten leather, then took them from the hook.

He sunk his hands deep into the gloves, then used his teeth to pull the strings tight. He went to the bedroom and chose an exterior wall he knew had brick behind the sheetrock, then started punching, softly at first, then harder. His big body, now older, was still strong. He remembered what one of his trainers had told him years before – that strength was the last thing to leave a fighter. First footwork leaves you, then speed, then strength. Over and over he punched at the wall. Short rights, left hook, uppercut into the air then back to the wall. He punched until he broke a full sweat, his knuckles aching inside the old leather. When he stopped he was out of breath. The clock said ten-thirty. He shook his hands from the gloves, threw them to the floor, then showered and lay on the bed. He stared at his red swollen fists and thought of the baby. Bender watched his enormous hands open and close as he'd watched the boy's tiny pink hands that day. He thought about Charlene and the smell of her hair in his face, her delicate hand in his, his hand running over her growing belly, and he waited for sleep. A full beer sat among the water stains.

That night he dreamed again, and again woke up with a vague feeling of having been cleansed, which quickly evaporated into the walls of the tiny room. The sheetrock on the wall Bender had punished the night before was broken. Cracks spidered out in every direction like a countryside map. A small pile of dust and broken bits of gypsum lay on the floor beneath his wallpaper foe.

In the kitchen, Bender stared at the telephone, trying to recall the number. He could not quite pull it up, but found his fingers knew which holes. Charlene answered.

"Hello?" she said.

Bender felt his heart go slack at the sound of her voice and he hung the receiver up. A feeling of utter loss enveloped him. Though it was only late morning, Bender walked to the bar. He saw that it was not yet open and kept walking. Without any idea of where he was going, Bender walked. His steps built a strange and somewhat comforting thrumming in his head. He was unaware of his surroundings. He could have been walking anywhere. He did not see the streets in front of him, the black birds watching him from telephone lines, the cars that lined the streets or the people he passed by. He was aware only of the soft humming in his head and the rhythmic beat of his own steps in his tattered work boots.

At a point, the soft thrum faded and Bender came back to himself. He took in his surroundings and it slowly came into view. He knew where he was – many miles from his small apartment. Bender turned a corner and saw the sign, still unlit, still hanging crookedly from rusted wire though he'd tried to straighten it many years prior. *Rochester Boxing Club*, it said. He eased the door open and walked in, his senses swamped by the familiar sounds and smells.

"Well, look who rose from the dead?"

"Hi Freddy."

"What the fuck are you doing here, old man Bender?"

"You got twenty years on me and you're still here."

"I never went away."

"True that. Freddy?"

"It's good to see you. I heard about Charlene and all that. I'm sorry, Ben."

"Freddy. I need something from you."

"What is it, Ben?"

"I just need to go a couple rounds."

"You don't even have your gloves. Look, you got work boots on, for Christ's sake."

"I don't even care who it is. Just put me in there for a couple."

"Bender, you were a good fighter and had some good game. Great chin – but Christ, you're fifty years old. The fuck you want to do this for?"

"I don't know, Freddy. I just need to. Forty-eight."

"I'll be honest with you, I ain't got anyone here today that can handle you. You're pushing, what, two-thirty?"

"You must have someone that just needs rounds. Just sparring, that's all I'm asking."

Bender outweighed the man by nearly forty pounds. He could see the trepidation in the young man's eyes, could feel the hesitation in his footwork – not wanting to close the distance. Then the young man connected and Bender let him. Freddy watched, arms folded, leaning in the door frame of his office. As his confidence came to him, the young man landed a few solid left jabs in Bender's face. A trickle of blood ran from Bender's nose. The young fighter closed in. Body, body, head. Bender allowed the other man to work him into the corner. He kept the borrowed gloves high, then lowered them slightly to lead the young man in closer. Bender threw just enough to lead the other fighter in, to make him think he had a fight on his hands, and something to prove.

"Christ, Ben…" muttered Freddy from across the room.

The young man pummeled Bender's face and body. Short straight rights, a looping left hook, body, body, head. Over and over, Bender took the punches, until the feeling of release from his dream came to him. The weight lifted. His nose, now broken, bled. A cut above his left eye opened up. He protected himself just enough to keep the beating going, as the darkness inside him lifted up and away and his strange atonement commenced. Inside his gloves, Bender curled his huge fists, weak and helpless as a newborn child's.

Primer Grey

So I been getting the old Pontiac ready for my kid lately. That's a good ride, a Pontiac. Been trying to find the original color even, but the code they give me don't look right. So I'm just gonna shoot a coat of primer for now. If I find that great old Pontiac green someday, I'll paint it up.

My kid? All his friends have those rodded-up Hondas. They sound like damn chainsaws. Drives me crazy. They're fast, yeah, but they got no power, you know? I mean real power. Now that old LeMans has got eight big pistons just banging away under that hood. That's what a car oughta sound like right there. So anyways, like I said, I been gettin' the Pontiac all fixed up for Charles.

I bought her new back in 71. Took every dime I had but I wanted it so damn bad. There was a bunch of good Pontiacs back then. I've always been a Pontiac man anyways. Coulda had a GTO. Coulda had a Ventura, but I like the LeMans best. My old man used to race, I guess that's what got me into cars. He was a hard man, my dad, and showy, you know? He was the kinda guy liked to make fun of everyone but couldn't take a joke about himself. He used to make fun of me in front of people. And he was a big guy, my old man, and tough too. Sometimes he'd smack me up side the head, "just on principle," he'd say. I never understood that. But it made me jumpy as hell around him, which I think was the point. "On principle" don't make any sense. He was just like that. That was his way. Kept my mom on her back foot too, but she was more careful than me I guess. He only smacked her a coupla times that I can remember.

Anyway, that's what got me into cars, my old man racing. He'd let me go with him on Sundays sometimes. I loved being around all those great cars. Loved the smell of it even. It gets in your blood. And my old man would win, too. He won quite a bit – now this is just regionals but still he got himself a trophy case and by god, he filled it up over the years. He was a Chevy guy, my old man. When I brought the LeMans home, he boxed me upside the head. Said I shoulda got a Chevelle and laughed. That was the last time he hit me. Said Pontiacs are for pussies. He never said nothing about how I saved all that money myself.

But I liked the Pontiacs, always did. Me and Lamere, we ran all over the place in that car. We went up to the mountains and even a couple times down to Boston. Got lost as all hell down there. Those Boston streets are confusing. Somebody told me it's because the roads follow old cow paths or something, but anyway, we didn't care. We had a great time in that car, me and Lemere. First time I went out with Arlene was in that car and you'd think that'd be a nice memory and maybe it is, but she's been on me for years to sell it, but I ain't gonna sell it.

Like I said, I been **gettin'** it all ready for Charles when he turns seventeen. New clutch plate, new shocks, the whole bit. Been finding what I need over at Emery's junkyard. They got a couple over there that I can pull from. They're way in back so it's a pain in the ass, but I take my time. One of 'em smells like skunk juice so I know the transmission is gone on it, but I got a decent flywheel and some other stuff from it. Arlene goes crazy when I come home with another part 'cause she knows I'll be on the creeper most of the weekend and won't go anywhere with her, but I wanna get it all back in good shape 'cause Charles turns seventeen soon, right? So I keep on with it.

Back when me and Lemere was running round, it was brand new. Had that great smell. I can close my eyes and remember that smell like it was today. I even had an eight-track under the dash and we'd listen to Foghat and Bad Company and I had almost all the Led Zeppelin tapes, too. We'd smoke a joint, not all the time, just once in awhile, you know, and have the best time. I raced it a few times too, 'cause later on I put a blower on it. It was fast. I never won in it but I didn't like driving it that hard anyways, so I stopped racing it.

The old man gave me some lip about that too, but I didn't care. I didn't want to take the chance of burning out the motor. He burned out motors all the time. It's like even though he was a Chevy man, he raced like he hated the car and wanted to burn it up. He was fast, my old man. Like I said, he filled that trophy case even if he never got past the regionals. He was a big talker too. It used to make me embarrassed. He always had to be the big man everywhere he went. I'd go to the races with him when he'd let me, but I'd run off and look at the Pontiacs as soon as I could get out of his sight. He was always telling everyone how he was gonna win and picking fights with the other drivers. Seemed to me you win bigger by not saying nothing about it then having a good race, but that's not how he was. And man, he'd get pissed when he lost, too. If he lost big, I knew I was in for it, almost like I was the one who raced him, you know? But this was way, way back when I was just a kid.

The car is starting to run real good. It's all tuned up and new brakes. Clutch is short and tight like it oughta be. Arelene, she's about had enough of me not going with her on the weekends and I tell her why I'm working so hard on it, for Charles, and she lightens up a little bit 'cause she thinks that's great too – how Charles is gonna have the Pontiac. I remind her about how our first date was in this car and she kind of gets a weird look in her eye like she's **some place** far off and I can tell she's thinking about something she don't want to say, so I just leave it there.

Like I was saying, Charles's friends all have those Hondas that they drop down. They get the suspension so tight you can hear 'em creak when they take a corner. And they can corner fast, that's true, but they ain't got the power like an old Pontiac. This one here is the 455 V8. That's some horsepower there and even though it's no good in the winter around here 'cause of the rear wheel drive, it's got the 4-speed manual trans so you can rock it if you get stuck. It's just a little squirrely on ice. So the day keeps getting nearer and Charles is gonna be seventeen and it's a big deal, of course, 'cause he'll be able to drive by himself. That's state law. You gotta be seventeen to drive by yourself. You can drive when you're sixteen but you gotta have someone with you. Me, I always liked driving alone, 'specially after I found out about Arlene and Lemere. But that's a long time ago.

So it gets to be Charles's birthday and I'm all excited. Arlene's pretty happy with Charles these days. He's doing better in school and he gets decent grades and overall he's a pretty good kid even though I know he's smoking dope, which I don't like, but he's doing better in school so I try to be grateful, you know? He's a good kid, never gave us much trouble. So Arlene, she gets him these gift cards 'cause she says Charles knows more about what he likes than we do and this way he can get all the things he likes at the stores he likes, even though he has to go all the way over to Indianapolis to the mall there. I guess she's smart that way – thinks things through.

So we have a nice morning and Charles likes the gift cards just like Arlene thought and it's all good and I say now I got a big surprise and I take him outside. I had put a red ribbon on the steering wheel the night before. So I say come with me, and he follows me around to the slab, and the car is there and all finished except for the paint job cause I can't find the right Pontiac green. And I hand him the keys and he's got this blank look on his face. And I tell him it's all his. Know what he says to me? I see him looking at it and something ain't right and then he says "How much you think I can get for it on a trade-in?" And for some weird reason all I can see is my old man's face, even though I'm looking right at Charles.

Take Home Pay

Danny Miller pulled a carpet knife from his back pocket with his right hand at the same time he wrapped the contractor around the neck with his left arm, so that when he pulled his weight back they both fell hard – the contractor landing on top of him, his back against Danny's front, staring up at the bright summer sky, the knife pressed against his throat. As the two men fell, a fat Mexican pushed forward and tried to make his way from the back seat of the Mercedes, but Eddie Cantrell stomped the door closed with a hard kick from his work boot and pointed his finger straight at the men in the back seat so they would not move, and they didn't.

"You'll cut another check, or I'll rip this fucking knife through you."

"It's a mistake."

"It's not my fucking mistake. I'm going to let you up. You're going to write another check for the full amount and those two guys are staying in the car. They try to get out of the car, I'm gonna cut you open. You tell them."

"Okay…"

The man didn't have to address the two in the back seat. They wanted no part of what was transpiring. The fat Mexican had only made a half-hearted attempt to get out of the car in the first place – more to make a show for his boss than to get involved. Danny loosened his left arm from around the contractor's neck, the man's face red from choking, and slid out and up from under the man before the contractor had fully righted himself. The contractor bent, hands on his knees, coughing hard for a moment, then stood straight and looked around for the book that had been knocked from his hand. The man was winded but other than that unmarked, except for a small red hyphen just under his Adam's apple. He found the leather covered check-book near the curb and leaned on the hood as he wrote.

"Don't come back," the contractor said.

"Don't worry about that, you fucking snake," Danny replied.

The contractor got in the car and pulled away slowly.

"We need to go now, before he puts a stop on it," said Danny.

"After that? He ain't gonna put a stop on shit. You almost killed that fucker."

"I hate these bastards. They think because they

skim off the Mexicans, they can skim us?"

"How much did he back charge?"

"Five hundred."

"Fuckin' A."

"Yeah."

Danny Miller and Eddie Cantrell loaded the stilts, step ladders, planks and hanging tools quickly into the faded green Ford pickup. They drew ties around the ladders and planks and pulled away from the job site. Across the street, a teenage girl watched them blankly from the huge bay window of her new home, a finger curling slowly in her brown hair. The pickup drove through the development, ignoring the speed limit and banged recklessly across each speed bump. When they reached the entrance gate, Danny turned right, heading towards Lubbock and the bank whose logo was on the check, instead of left towards Amarillo and his apartment and his own bank.

"You're gonna have to go, you know," Eddie said. A statement, not a question.

"I've had enough anyway."

"Me too. It's been 15 years and we're getting the same board price we was back then."

"Yup."

Danny's left arm was weak, aching from the strain, and his hands were shaking slightly as the

43

adrenaline started to have its way. He held the
steering wheel tightly with both hands, his knuckles
white, so that Eddie wouldn't notice. He scanned the
rear view mirror every few seconds, just in case. They
drove into the parking lot of the bank and pulled
over. Danny took the check from his wallet, signed
it, drove up to the drive-through, cashed the check
and the two men were on their way within a minute.
As they exited the parking lot, the contractor's
Mercedes pulled in, the car nearly touching the side
of Danny's truck as they passed close. Eddie leaned
and shot a middle finger from across the bench seat,
but the contractor didn't look up.

The pair drove north toward Amarillo, stopping
only to fill the tank, each buying a 12-pack of beer
and a barbecue sandwich at the gas station in Tulia.
Danny took 87 instead of the Interstate to avoid the
state troopers who occasionally stopped work trucks
like his for minor offences and so that they could
search for drugs. Danny also had it in the corner of
his mind that it was possible the contractor had
called them in, though he knew Eddie was right. The
Mexicans weren't about to witness and it was most
likely done and dusted as long as they didn't go back
to Lubbock anytime soon. Somewhere just past
Happy, Texas, where 87 turned slightly west away

from the Interstate, Eddie pointed east out his window.

"Look."

"Revival?"

"Yeah. Big one."

In the distance, blue and white bunting danced a wicked jig in the wind. Large conical speakers hung from tall poles, their honk and bleat barely heard above the road noise. A hundred or so people sat in folding chairs. A few stood waving their arms ecstatically, some waved from their seats. The preacher was in full blood with fists high in the air; he screeched into the microphone in rhythmic waves of words. Each proclamation had the same rhythm and each looked more dramatic than the previous. A sign was nailed to a rancher's gate: 'Revival This Weekend' hand-painted in red letters.

"He looks like Jerry Lee Lewis," said Eddie.

"Probably lives like him."

"Think he's married to his cousin?"

"If he is, he's found the Bible passage says he can."

"They got a way of twisting that stuff."

"They got a way of back charging, too."

"Don't doubt that. Everybody's back charging somebody."

Back at his apartment, Danny was restless and upset somewhere inside he couldn't place. He tried to watch television but the voices irritated him, so he shut it off and tried to read a magazine, but found himself reading the same part over and over so gave up on that as well. He pulled the tab on a third Lone Star and sat staring out the kitchenette window from his one kitchen chair. He thought about Becky and wondered where she was and how it had gone wrong. He thought about the time when he had visited her at the doctor's office where she was the receptionist and she had led him back into the examination room and taken him in her mouth. He thought about all the cheap things he had done to her and the lousy ways he had treated her and he let it fill him until his guilt and self-loathing felt good, then he kept thinking until the good feeling turned into something dark.

Outside the apartment, the parking lot was filled with the laughter of children, the shouts of mothers calling them home, and pleas for just a bit more time. The long horizon darkened slowly from pink then orange to deep purple and the twelve-minute sky held back the coming night. Danny fell asleep in a DAV armchair as the children's voices faded, and then he was filled with fitful dreams.

Demons shouted curses at him. Black horned things with impossibly long fingers like the branches of trees clawed at him. A deep well opened at his feet and he found himself standing at the precipice of a great void. Preachers – naked, blind, bleached white and hairless – ranted gibberish into his ears as he strained to hear, panicked, to make sense of their words. Above him, black clouds flew by in fast-forward. He lost his balance and fell forward into an endless depth. The open mouths of the screaming preachers followed him as he fell forever down.

When Danny woke it was barely morning, the sun having just crested the horizon. He brushed the acrid night from his mouth, rinsing a few extra times, and he felt a strange darkness in himself. He stared into his own eyes in the bathroom mirror until, completely unsettled, he turned away. He felt as if he was both himself and someone else. As though his dream-self had woken with him and inside him. The carpet knife was on the metal kitchen table where he had left it. He took the knife with its hooked blade and ran his thumb across the edge. It was sharper than he expected for a knife that saw so much use. He slipped it under the newspaper that was on the table so that he wouldn't have to see it.

Danny made a full pot of coffee and fried two

eggs. He stood over the toaster and smelled the electric heating elements as they browned the bread then slopped the eggs between the toast and ate it as a sandwich at the kitchen door, sipping strong black coffee between bites. His thoughts turned to Becky again, but not to the doctor's office.

This time he thought about when they had first met and how he'd been embarrassed about the tobacco in his lip and the plastic soda bottle into which he'd been spitting the thick brown liquid. He remembered trying to figure out how to get the tobacco from his mouth without her seeing, mortified to be holding a bottle of his own refuse. They'd met at a party held by a friend of a friend and Danny had been nervous and jittery trying to speak with her, finally summoning the courage to ask to see her again before leaving the party with his stomach in knots. They'd had a decent enough run of it until he had made a mess of things by sleeping with a waitress one night when he was working out of town. He'd been feeling down and let the waitress pursue him, agreeing to meet her at a bar near the job site after work. He'd fucked her on the bench seat of the pick-up truck out in the parking lot, the door open, Danny standing in the gravel drive, the waitress still wearing her top, her skirt on the floorboard of his truck. After they finished, the woman left in her own car and Danny had gotten sick in the parking lot, knowing what he'd done and already knowing that he would tell Becky. He tried telling himself he might not tell her in an effort to keep from being sick again when he got back to the hotel. He remembered the rawness of his emotions and the thought of what he'd done and felt queasy all over again. It somehow felt good to think about this horrible thing he'd done and what a shit he'd been, as it helped to have a reason she was no longer with him. Her clothes were no longer sharing his closet, her hairbrush with its sweet smell no longer in his bathroom, her lovely tanned limbs no longer stretched out in his bed. It helped make sense of things to know he deserved to be where he was, alone in his shit-hole apartment.

Danny showered, dressed, brushed his teeth, then walked out onto the shared balcony of his apartment. The sun narrowed his eyes and gave him a headache. The sky was exploding with light and belted down on his eyes. He got in his truck and drove from the parking lot, silently cursing the children on their bicycles for intentionally being slow to get out his way. The dreams seemed to stay with him and he couldn't fully shake the bad feeling in the pit of his stomach. He knew he'd been reckless with the contractor and felt both his seething anger at the man and at the same time embarrassment that he'd come so close to hurting someone over money. In his mind, he could not find the place where his anger and embarrassment met. There seemed to be no way out of the trouble, which started his anger rising yet again at the contractor for putting him in that position.

On this cycle went as he drove aimlessly, feeling the warm air across his brown forearm where it rested on the truck door. Danny drove south – retracing, without thinking, his route from the day before. Thirty minutes later, just outside Happy, Texas, he saw the banners and the blue and white bunting waving wildly at him. He pulled the truck to the shoulder and cut the engine. For a long while, he sat still in the truck, the sun refracting cruelly through the windshield and extracting a full sweat from his body. The dreams ran in his mind like a film, but visceral; he could feel the strange preachers' mouths against his ear and could see the horrible visions. When he tried closing his eyes, the scenes became more vivid. His stomach was queasy. He thought again about the contractor and both shame and anger rose to a head. Danny sat long enough to sweat through his t-shirt, then got out of the truck, waited for a passing semi, and crossed the road to the revival. He felt his self-consciousness rise as he neared the group, smaller today than yesterday, and the hairs on his neck raised as he got near enough to hear the preacher's words in the hanging speakers.

"There's thousands of people gonna die tonight across the world. Thousands of those people are not gonna be ready to meet God. That's why I read you this first thing that God told me – that God called you and touched you for a reason that you can touch somebody else. And if we don't start touching people, don't worry 'bout the word cause God said he hastens the word to perform it. And I didn't have anybody in that room with me in that little room but a little bitty Bible about that high and that big and that's all I had to read was the New Testament. But the Bible says any man can cometh unto me and no-wise I shall not cast him out. And I said, 'God, if you want to see a picture of me, I make a Hell's Angel look good!' I'm really telling you the truth. I was a miserable looking beast!"

Calls of "Amen" came from the crowd. No one looked at Danny as he approached, their eyes either cast down or trained on the sweating preacher.

"And God did a transformation on me, so

much that I had my dad take me over to my mother's house on the way to church and all my family was on the porch and they didn't recognize me! They didn't know who I was. That was God's transformation! And there's thousand will die tonight to spend the rest of eternity burning in hell!"

Sweat poured from his forehead, the collar of his thin polyester jacket was dark blue and wet down to his chest. When the preacher raised the Bible high to accentuate his words, Danny could see the man's armpits were soaked down to the bottom hem.

He sat in a grey folding metal chair at the back of the crowd and listened. Across the field, the land was dead flat. Whispers of dirt rose up threatening to form devils, spun for a moment, then lay back down again. The sound of the preacher's voice was sharp and rhythmic from the speakers overhead.

"And all they had to do was say Jesus come into my heart, I accept you as my savior...I want to be born again!"

The preacher roared along and Danny began to feel his troubling dreams lifting from his mind. He felt a cold chill in his neck and the hairs on his arms raised. His eyes were wet before he knew it and his knees moved up and down involuntarily, his chest billowed in small wracks. He could feel himself crying softly and could not stop himself, though he felt no particular embarrassment. No one paid him any mind and he continued crying, not truly trying to stop and only somewhat even aware of himself. The dreams floated up and away from him and he felt their release. He felt his anger leave him too. Across the field more dust devils spun up and out.

"You know what you become? A brand new creation, a brand new creature. I'm talking about a creation of God. He's the Lord God Almighty if we know him well and know him rightly…"

The preacher kept on, and the sun did as well as it moved slowly in its summer arc across the sky. The man talked for hours. Danny's crying softened and he found himself immobile, the air around him filled with the man's words. The words sounded beautiful to him, the enormous blue sky yawned wider than he'd ever seen, and his body felt un-tethered and limp.

As the preacher started to bring his unceasing sermon to a close, a young boy in a starched white short-sleeve shirt emerged from behind the makeshift pulpit with a shoe box in his hands. The boy made his way across and down the rows stopping fully in front of each person, pushing the box in front of them and looking directly at them, awaiting each donation. The boy stood achingly long in front of some of the faithful, the box extended in front of him. As the boy moved, the preacher's eyes followed along with him and he exhorted directly toward whomever the boy stood in front of. The bills continued to pile into the box and when they reached the top, the boy pushed them down again to make room. When the boy reached Danny, he pulled his wallet from his jeans and emptied the contents, a feeling of exaltation coursing through him. Looking up, the preacher's gaze buried deep into his own.

"The wicked borroweth, and payeth not again! Well, if you don't pay your taxes, sorry, I'm not twisting it – you are wicked...otherwise get some scissors and start cutting these verses out, but don't carry a Bible that you say you believe in and then debit to follow if you don't intend ever to take every single word of that book be you doers of the word and not hearers only – deceiving your own selves!"

The boy finished collecting from the last row, then walked briskly back to the stage and behind it, the back of his shirt clinging to his sweaty neck.

Danny sat still as the crowd murmured amens, some of them speaking softly to themselves, most with eyes cast down toward the dirt at their feet as they rose and left slowly. He did not move. When the last of them had made their way to their cars, Danny finally stood in the quiet. He could hear the plastic bunting slapping softly against the wooden poles and the low electrical hum of the muted speakers. He made his way down through the parade of folding chairs, a wonderful heavy feeling filling his chest. When he neared the back of the stage, he heard the preacher's voice, now soft and raspy from his work.

"I'm going to have to back charge you, son. You worked them too quick; there should be more here."

Store Bought

When Christmas came, it was more hand-me-downs, and Les's heart sank. He'd been hoping for a new pair of sneakers. The other kids had started the school year with brand-new clothes. Most of the boys had bright sneakers; the girls, shining patent leather black and white saddle shoes. Les had been eyeing a pair of blue nylon Jox all the long months between the start of the school year and Christmas break. Les did his best to hide his disappointment and told his parents it was the best Christmas ever.

Les's father, Ted, worked at the shoe factory in town. The factory did not make sneakers but made work boots and women's shoes of various styles. Les's mother, Polly, ironed dresses for well-to-do women who lived in the lovely old Craftsman and Victorian homes that lined the streets in town. At Christmas there were hand-me-downs from his cousins, and clothes from the thrift store, and a few very cheap trinkets from the dollar store downtown.

The family lived in a crumbling salt-box house at the edge of town. The dirt floor cellar flooded every spring and Les spent many nights with his father bailing it out with buckets, in a hail of his father's curses. Every year, when the rains came, his father swore there would be a sump pump the following year, but with each rainy season, there was no sump pump.

He had first seen the sneakers on a shopping trip with his mother. Polly shopped at various stores, always looking for the best buy: groceries were cheapest at Sawyer Mills, sundries cheapest at Seigel's department store a few miles over the border. Their own small town in Maine had sales tax, so Polly shopped in New Hampshire which had none. His mother had been running through her shopping list and let Les wander the store while she shopped. The sneakers were electric blue with red and white stripes across the top. When he first picked them up, he was surprised at how light they were. He thought to himself how fast he might run in them. He pictured himself wearing them in gym class and remembered a day when a boy had pointed at his ratty Keds.

"Those are girl sneakers."

"No, they're not."

"Look, Les has girl sneakers," the boy laughed and others joined in.

He imagined himself with the fancy shoes sticking out from under his desk in Mr. Carter's sixth grade class. Les had even showed them to his mother before leaving the store, hoping to plant in her the idea of his having them for school that year.

"Those are very pretty," said his mother.

"They're not pretty. They're fast, mom," Les said.

"They're very expensive."

"They're only a little more than the regular ones."

"A little more is *not* what we have, Les."

"What if I did more chores?"

"Les, we can't afford these. You know that."

But the thought of the blue sneakers had rooted in his mind and would not leave, even after he started sixth grade wearing a used pair of dirty Keds handed down from a cousin. Whenever Polly went shopping that fall, Les tagged along and found his way to the shoe department to covet the sneakers again.

After the Christmas presents were opened, Polly gathered the wrapping paper up, flattened each piece, and refolded it into neat squares, which she saved in a cardboard box in the attic for the following Christmas. Les tried hard to not let his disappointment show and thanked his parents for such a wonderful Christmas, but in his mind all he could see were the blue sneakers.

"Les, I need your help this afternoon," Ted said.

"On Christmas?"

"The driveway doesn't know it's Christmas, and it needs shoveling."

"But the special shows are on TV, dad."

"You'll see them after we shovel."

"Can't we have it plowed like everybody else?"

His father fell silent and Les felt bad for protesting.

"I'll get my boots on, dad. I've seen the first ones last year, anyway."

Les went to the bread bag drawer and rummaged to find a matching pair of bags to slip over his socks before putting his feet into his hand-me-down snowmobile boots. The felt inside the boots crumbled slightly each time he put them on and he felt the small pieces under his feet as he put on his winter parka and knitted mittens. He followed his father outside and they began shoveling the long steep driveway.

On the first day after Christmas break, Les saw that many of the other kids wore new parkas, new snowmobile boots and new clothing as well. His friend Danny had a t-shirt with the Jaws movie logo on it, a shark's head with its menacing black eyes and white teeth and the film's title in big letters at the top. All the boys thought it was the best. The kids traded stories of their Christmas gifts, each trying to up the ante with a bigger gift than the last. Les avoided the buzzing conversations, feeling a deep awkwardness inside and a small but potent jealousy in his heart. He looked over at Brenda Bodden who sat silent at her desk. He remembered that Brenda was a Jehovah's Witness, and that they did not celebrate Christmas. He watched her from the corner of his eye, wondering what she felt and feeling some small and strange connection. After a few days back in school, things returned to normal and the excitement dwindled to a small glow, for which Les was grateful.

When spring break arrived, the trees burst into a verdant growth. At night Les's bones ached and he found himself with a temper he'd not known before and strained to control. His parents understood and let out a bit of line in small ways, that he might more comfortably feel his way to his looming independence. For the first time, they allowed Les free rein on his secondhand one-speed Schwinn bicycle. Les spent the spring break ranging across the small town into neighborhoods that were new and exciting to ride through. He still thought about the sneakers.

On the second Saturday of the spring vacation, Les rode his bike across town, crossed the short bridge to the New Hampshire line, then kept riding along the gravelly side of the two-lane highway for several miles, until he found himself in the parking lot of the Seigel's department store where he had first seen the electric blue sneakers. In the parking lot, he found a plastic bag, which he shook out and wiped clean on the leg of his trousers, then stuffed into his back pocket. Having no kickstand, he leaned his bike against the back side of the building and went around the corner and into the store. He went to the shoe department. The blue sneakers were still displayed in a prominent position on one of the endcaps. Les's hands were shaking lightly and he felt his face was flushed. His t-shirt was wet at his armpits. He told himself he hadn't done it yet, and that he didn't have to, and this calmed him slightly. He told himself he was just trying them on. He scanned through the boxes until he found his own size, eight, then slipped the box from the pile and put the sneakers on his feet. A clerk turned the corner at the endcap.

"Can I help you with something?" said the clerk.

"No, I'm just looking at these sneakers."

"Are you finding your size?"

"I think so."

"Here, let me check." She squatted in front of Les and pinched the toe of the blue nylon sneaker. "Yes, that feels about right, but you might want to go up just a half size. You don't have much room to grow there. Let me see if we have a half size up." The clerk scanned the boxes then slid another out; the boxes above it dropped down in a cardboard thud. "Let's try these. An eight and a half." Les sat still on the bench, his heart racing. The clerk untied the sneakers on his feet.

"Slip those off and let's see if we can get you just a bit more room to grow."

Les used the heel of one sneaker to push the other sneaker off, then his toe to push off the first sneaker. He looked down at his stained socks, a small hole worn into the side of one of them, and his face flushed with embarrassment. His hands were shaking so he pressed them at his sides on the bench so that the clerk wouldn't notice. The clerk slid the sneakers onto his feet. They felt wonderful. She tied them up and pushed at the toe again. Even sitting still, Les could feel how light they were.

"Why don't you walk around for a bit and see how those feel? I'll be back to check on you in a few minutes. Let me help this other customer find what they are looking for."

As soon as the clerk turned the corner, Les started towards the door. He tried to tell himself to slow down, that he needed to act casual, and so he reeled himself in as much as he could. He could feel the plastic bag bulging in his back pocket. This was better. How was he going to get the bag past the check out anyway? This way he could simply walk out. If he was caught, he could even say he forgot to put his own sneakers back on. As all this raced through his mind, he suddenly found himself outside the store, the electric blue sneakers on his feet. He ran and cornered the building, grabbed his bicycle and pedaled furiously with a hot pounding in his chest. An enormous smile plastered his face. He kept the pace until he reached the two-lane highway that led back to the border, then he coasted for a bit, out of breath.

When he reached home, Les realized he had a conundrum – how to explain the sneakers? He put his Schwinn away in the garage and took off the sneakers and socks. He wrapped the blue sneakers carefully in a clean rag, then stuffed the sneakers into the empty ash collector beneath the pot-belly stove that his father lit in the winter when he needed to work on the car or fix some other broken thing. He went inside barefoot.

"Where are your shoes and socks?" Polly asked.

"It was so warm, I just went barefoot, mom. You know I like to go barefoot."

"It's 60 degrees out. Hardly warm enough to go barefoot. Where have you been?"

"I was just riding around. It's been great since you and dad let me go past Emery's Bridge. It's real nice out today."

"Well, you put socks and shoes on if you go out again. You'll catch a cold and we don't need a doctor bill or you missing school."

"Okay, mom."

"You're awfully chipper today. Where's the moody Les?"

"It was just so nice out today."

"Are you excited about your birthday?"

"Sure. I'm excited. I'm gonna go listen to records now."

"Do you know what you want for your birthday?"

"Oh, you always get me something great. I'm gonna listen to records now."

"Why the rush? Don't you have anything special you might want for your birthday? Have you made a list?"

"No. I'll be happy with anything. Maybe a new record. I like that Jim Stafford song, *Spiders and Snakes*."

"Okay. Well, we'll see what happens."

On Monday morning Les wore his boots out to the garage, changed into the electric blue sneakers, and rode his bike to school. He felt fast, strong and good. A few of the boys at school commented on his sneakers and inside he flushed with pride. His friend Danny stuttered that they were "wicked cool" which he said as "Wwwwiiiicked Ccccool, Les." Les felt disappointed that he had to wait until Friday for gym class to really see what the sneakers could do. When school was out for the day, he rode his bike home, removed the sneakers, wrapped them in the rag and returned them to their hiding place in the ash collector. He put on his boots and went inside. At dinner he found he had a difficult time talking with his parents. He felt a bit out of sorts.

"So the big thirteen is coming up this weekend," Ted said. "That's a big deal. You'll be a teenager."

"Yeah," said Les.

"Well, aren't you excited?"

"Yeah." Les pushed his food around his plate.

"Oh, it's this Les today, is it?" Polly asked.

"I just don't feel too good."

"Prob'ly 'cause you were riding that bike around in bare feet this weekend. I hope you're not sick." Polly reached her hand over the table and felt his forehead. "You don't feel hot," she said.

"No, I'm okay. Can I be excused?"

"Yes. Why are you wearing your winter boots?"

"Oh, no reason. Lots of the guys are still wearing them. It's kind of cool."

Each day Les changed from boots to sneakers to boots again. Each day he felt a growing discomfort inside. Across the days, the thrill of the electric blue sneakers slowly faded, until it sat in his stomach as a boiling guilty pain.

On Saturday morning, Les came downstairs to find his parents already up and in the kitchen. Red balloons filled the table and there was an enormous box, wrapped in Christmas paper, sitting on the table between the plates that were set for breakfast.

"Happy Birthday, young man!" Polly said. "I'm making you your favorite breakfast and we have a special gift for you!"

Polly stood at the stove waiting to flip the blueberry pancakes. Link sausages simmered on the back burner.

"Thirteen. Practically a man. We're very proud of you," said Ted

"Go ahead, open it!" Polly said.

Les carefully pulled the recycled Christmas wrapper away from the box, trying not to tear it. Inside the enormous box was another box, also wrapped in Christmas paper. He pulled the smaller box out and carefully pulled the paper from it as well. Les lifted the top of the box. The electric blue sneakers stared up at him.

"This is a very special birthday, Les. We're so proud of who you are and what a fine young man you're becoming, so we've been saving for months. You thought I forgot all about it, but I knew how much you wanted these. I took on some extra ironing from a friend of Mrs. Kenny. Do you love them? We're so excited to get you something you really want for once, Les."

Les stared down at the shoes and felt his stomach twist into a vicious knot.

Medicine Man

Roger had been having trouble sleeping for weeks. He'd tried a few solutions, none of which had worked. For a while, he tried drinking exactly two glasses of red wine before bed each night. He had read in an online article that two glasses of red wine was the exact amount of alcohol, and the preferred type of alcohol, to encourage a full night's sleep. But the wine had not worked. Roger also tried Sominex, Unisom, and Aleve PM. When they all failed him, he spent a few days taking nothing and then tried Melatonin, which did nothing as well. The longer his insomnia went on, the more ravaged he felt during the day and the more desperate he was for sleep. On the weekend, he tried making up for his sleepless hours by napping, but found that it made falling asleep at the day's end even more difficult. So Roger swore off napping. He tried masturbating before going to bed, but while it helped him to fall asleep he found he would fully wake again a few hours later to the soft ticking of his clock.

Sometimes when Roger woke in the night, he would try to read to feel sleepy again. Sometimes he watched television, but found neither would allow him to sleep through the night. During the day, he found himself so exhausted that he would feel a strange sense of being both asleep and awake. The feeling disturbed him greatly and he found it frightening. Several times, on his way home from his job at the insurance agency, he'd suddenly jolted awake behind the steering wheel to the honking of the car behind him, his car braked to a stop at a stop sign or green light. He had even fallen asleep at his desk at work. He'd almost been caught several times by the office manager, who had the habit of knocking but not waiting for a response before walking into his tidy office.

Roger was desperate for sleep. When he woke in the middle of the night, a feeling of fear and anxiety raced through his mind and he felt panicked. Sometimes he would turn the clock around to face the other way so that when he woke he would not know what time it was. He didn't want to know that he'd only slept three hours.

As the weeks went by, his appearance started to change. He developed deep, dark circles under his eyes and he appeared to age as well, stooping just slightly in his exhaustion. His work was beginning to suffer, and the other insurance men would ask, "Are you feeling okay?"

"Oh yes, I just need to catch up on my sleep a little bit. Been burning the candle at both ends. You know..." Roger would say.

"Oh, sure. I was single once too," they'd say.

Night after night, it went on and on. He'd fall asleep watching television or reading, only to re-wake every night at roughly three AM. Sometimes he would become very upset and attempt to talk himself back to calmness. Sometimes he would get up and pour a wine or whiskey out of desperation. Sometimes he'd stare out one of the bedroom windows in a sort of trance – half asleep, half awake.

Eventually, Roger was so worn down that he made an appointment with his physician.

"Yes, I can see that you are worn out, Roger," his doctor told him.

"Is there anything you can prescribe that's safe?" Roger asked.

Roger was very careful about prescriptions and wasn't much of a drinker. He had turned to the wine and whiskey only out of desperation. Working in insurance, Roger knew the addiction risks of prescription medications but he was at wits' end.

"I'm going to prescribe Trazodone, Roger," said his doctor. "It's quite a potent drug, so I'm going to start you at a low dose and then we'll see from there."

"Is it safe?"

"Well, you must be careful not to mix it with alcohol; like I said, it's quite potent, but as long as you take it as prescribed and don't mix it with any other medications, you should be fine."

"Okay. I'll be careful," Roger said. Roger was always careful.

Later that night, Roger prepared himself for bed. He felt a glimmer of hope that the Trazodone might work and that he might finally sleep through the night. He brushed his teeth, flossed, washed his face, then opened the small medicine bottle. He took out one small pill and downed it with a small glass of water then went to lie in his bed. He pulled the covers back just the way he liked – at a perfect triangle – and lay down and waited. An hour later he felt the glorious pull of sleep swimming in his head. He looked at his alarm clock – eleven PM. If the pill worked, he could possibly get seven hours of sleep – more than he'd had in weeks. At three AM, Roger woke. He'd been in a very deep sleep, could not remember his dreams, and felt a profound disappointment at finding himself awake again. Then he had a thought. If one pill had given him three good hours of sleep perhaps he could take another, wait the hour for it to kick in, then get another three hours of sleep. So Roger got up, went to the bathroom, fumbled with the bottle, then took another tiny pill.

When Roger woke, he reached for the alarm clock and discovered that it was eight AM and he was a bit late. Frantically, he dressed, brushed his teeth, flossed and flew out the door as quickly as he could. He drove fast, trying to make up time, but calculated that he would be late for work regardless, and he was. Roger pulled into the parking lot of Trousdale Insurance & Casualty Company, found a parking spot, and tried to calm himself. He'd never been late to work before. Roger was ever a cautious man. He straightened his tie, checked his hair in the rearview mirror, and went into the office.

"Well, look who decided to show up," his boss, Ned Trousdale said.

"Yes, I'm sorry, Ned."

"We have a phoner at ten with Thomas."

"I'll be ready. I organized everything yesterday."

"Very good. Are you okay, Roger?"

"Yes, yes. Been having a bit of trouble sleeping lately, that's all."

"Ah, the single life."

"Yeah, the single life."

Roger went into his office and hurried to organize his notes for the phone meeting; his head was still swimming from the Trazodone.

At the end of the day, Roger drove home exhausted. He usually listened to the news, weather and traffic reports on the radio, but he found the voices irritated him in his uncomfortable state. When he arrived home, he collapsed on the sofa and fell into a deep sleep. On waking, he found that he'd slept until nine PM and felt a surge of panic. He wondered how he would ever sleep again that night. Roger made a sandwich for dinner, brushed and flossed, laid his clothes out for the following day, set two of the tiny pills on his nightstand, and lay staring at the ceiling. The soft ticking of the turned-around clock filled the room. He thought to himself that his mistake the night before was that he'd taken the pills too far apart, so he decided that he would take two of the pills together, and so he did. A few hours later, Roger felt the sweet pull of sleep again and at two AM he was again in a deep sleep. Strange, vivid dreams came to him, swinging wildly through his head. He saw his deceased parents in an argument over a broken dish. He saw his ex-wife yelling to him from an ivy-covered balcony, but when he tried to answer her, he was mute. He was chased by a dark shadow through an abandoned metal building – the heat unbearable in there. On and on the dreams ricocheted around his mind, his eyes twitching rapidly beneath his closed red lids.

In spite of the sleep, when he woke, Roger found himself more exhausted than ever. He turned the clock around to see the time, though the window shade told him it was not yet morning. Five AM. He dragged his body to the bathroom and stared into the mirror. His eyes were swollen and red and a deeper, darker shade had taken hold in the soft skin beneath them. He stared for a long time, disturbed and a bit unraveled by his reflection. The bottle of Trazodone sat on the counter. Looking at it, he felt angry. Roger went to the kitchen and turned on the coffee maker. He did not consider seeking more sleep or the bottle. It was too late into the morning to force himself back to sleep with the pills, so he sat on the avocado green sofa and sipped the black coffee waiting for the caffeine to come to him while he watched the morning news. He felt the weight of his eyelids.

At work that day, Roger found his mind cloudy. It was difficult to focus and to keep at the task at hand. He was grateful there were no meetings, but still there were policies to go over, decisions to be made, and a small and growing mountain of papers to address.

"Roger?" said the office manager. "Roger? Are you feeling okay?"

Roger sat upright at his desk, pen in hand.

"What?"

"Roger, you don't look right. Are you feeling okay?"

"Yes, I'm okay. I'm just feeling a bit dragged down."

"You don't look right. Do you think you should see a doctor?"

"Oh no. I'm fine. Just a bit dragged down, like I said."

"Well, we need those Rockingham County reports by the end of the day."

"Oh yes, they'll be finished. I'm getting to them now. I have all the numbers."

"If you need help, just ask. You really don't look right. I don't mean that the way it sounds but honestly, you don't seem right."

"I can't sleep."

"Oh, that's hard. I go through it once in awhile myself."

"Have you found anything that helps?"

"A glass of red wine. Sometimes I take a Benadryl."

At the day's end, Roger handed the neat stack of three-hole-punched reports to the office manager, then left the building and went to his car. He sat in the driver's seat, closed his eyes and quickly fell asleep. When he woke, the parking lot was empty. Panicked, Roger checked his phone for the time and saw that it was nearly eleven PM. His mind raced. Had anyone seen him sleeping in his car? He started the Honda and raced home, flushed with embarrassment. At home, he undressed, laid out his clothes for the next day, then took three of the small pills. He lay in bed thinking about his ex-wife. He remembered watching her sleep and her soft breathing. He reached for himself but there was no response and so he gave up. Hours drifted by as he lay staring at the ceiling. A soft pull lulled him into a trance, but again he did not sleep. Too tired for anger, Roger simply lay in his bed, his impossibly heavy eyelids half shut as his mind wandered from memory to memory. All night long, he simply lay there in his trance.

The next morning, Roger made his coffee extra strong. It was Friday finally, and he told himself that he could push through the day, that he could rally for one more day then reassess his predicament on the weekend. He brushed his teeth, flossed and dressed with a pounding in his head. The morning news chattered from the television.

At work, he poured a stale cup from the grimy office coffee maker and went to his office. He sat in his chair, put his forehead against the desk and promptly fell fully asleep. There was a knock on his door and Ned walked in.

"Roger?"

His head still rested on the desk. A small bit of saliva ran from his lower lip.

"Roger."

Roger woke, startled, and looked frantically around the room not knowing where he was.

"Jesus Christ, Roger, are you okay?"

"Oh, Ned. I'm so sorry. I finished the reports yesterday. Everything is fine."

"I saw the reports. They don't make much sense. Is everything okay? You always do such good work. You're never late. I always count on you but something doesn't seem right. Maybe you're partying a bit too much, eh?"

"Well, you know the bachelor life, Ned."

"Well, you need to get yourself together. Those reports don't make sense. We have a meeting with corporate on Monday and they need to be redone. You're going to have to either hustle today to redo them or come in this weekend. They're a mess."

"Sorry, Ned. I'll get right on it."

"Do you need to see a doctor?"

"Oh, no. I'll pull it together."

Roger shuddered at the thought of having to spend his Saturday back at the office. He retrieved the reports from the office manager's desk. As he looked them over, he saw that indeed they made no sense: he had used the wrong numbers. He would need to start from scratch on them, and so he did. Roger drank cup after cup of the bitter office coffee and pushed through the reports as quickly as he could while telling himself to focus. At the day's end, he had completed his task and felt both a huge rush of relief and the full weight of his fatigue pushing down on him. His head was pulsing with a headache and he could feel hot blood pounding in his head with every heartbeat. Roger gave the new reports to the office manager, making sure that she understood the reports had been redone and that she should ensure she gave Ned the new reports and not confuse them with original reports he had turned in.

Roger said his goodbyes for the weekend and went to his car. He started the engine and let the cool from the air conditioner blow over him, which eased his pounding head slightly. After closing his eyes for a few moments, he put the car in gear and drove home.

When Roger woke the next morning, he realized that he had finally slept through the night. He did not remember driving home, or if he'd taken any of the small pills, but he was so grateful for the sleep that he said a small prayer. His headache was gone. Roger made coffee, put out the makings for breakfast and turned on the television set to watch the morning news. He sat on the green sofa and felt wonderful sipping his coffee, the smell of cooking bacon hanging in the air. The local news predicted rain for the weekend, but Roger was unbothered as he had nothing planned save for a short trip to the grocery. There was a report of a hit and run that killed a bicycling twelve-year old child. The child's crying mother pleaded for information in a short unhinged interview; the wrecked bright-red bicycle sat in the background in a twisted knot of metal. The program then went to the national segment and the week's financial news, and Roger ate his breakfast curled comfortably into the crook of the avocado green sofa.

After finishing his breakfast, Roger decided to make his grocery run so he could be done with it. He would spend the weekend watching films and reading, he thought. He was still filled with relief that he had finally slept, and felt certain that the ordeal was over and that he'd broken the spell. Roger brushed his teeth, flossed, dressed in comfortable weekend clothes, and went out to his car. As he opened the driver's side door, something caught his eye at the front corner of the Honda. He walked around the open door and on the front quarter panel Roger saw a large dent and bright-red paint etched into his silver car. A long and deep red scrape ran from the bumper all the way to the side view mirror. He stood very still and stared at the red paint as it came to him.

Blanket of Stars

She had heard about him from girls at school.
He was back from the Marines, the brother of the
one with the greasy hair and leathery smell who sat
two rows in front of her in civics class, the boy who
couldn't keep his mouth shut, always with some
obvious wisecrack. She had heard about how
beautiful he was, heard about his tattoos, blonde hair
and chiseled arms. He had a Chevy that he told
everyone was salmon colored, though it looked pink
to her, sitting in the parking lot at Barbados Pond.
She had listened to all that kind of talk before from
her melodramatic girlfriends – going on about movie
stars and Elvis and this one and that one. Though
she played along, inside her head she always found
the boys her friends went on about dull and distant.
How could you know if you liked a boy from a
photograph anyway?

She wasn't expecting him to be all that
handsome and his hair to be all that golden, his arms
all that chiseled, and for him to be beautiful. But he
was. He arrived with three loud and rough friends,
though he himself didn't seem to be all that rough

and he was not loud. She thought she saw them sneaking sips of beer and she didn't like that, but it did seem brave in a way. Alcohol was strictly forbidden at Barbados Pond. She'd never seen anyone flaunt that rule since this was the one and only place to cool off in the entire Strafford County area. The pond wasn't big, but the whole park itself was expansive enough to handle every teenager with enough nerve to bare skin and risk an occasional dunking from some over-torqued senior. He was tanned already though it was only June. She wondered where the Marines had sent him and if they had sent him someplace where he had been sitting in the sun the last few months, because he was brown tanned like at the end of summer, not red tanned like the beginning of summer. She wasn't close enough to make out exactly what his tattoos were. She thought they looked angry, but mostly they looked dirty. Still, he was beautiful and his hair was golden just like they had gushed in the hallway; "Oh my god, guess who is back from the Marines?"

He drank long from a brown paper bag and put the bag back inside the driver's side floorboard of the pink Chevy. His eyes were impossibly blue, she thought, and she had never seen exactly and precisely that blue before. There's no blue like that in the

Crayola box, she thought. With his noisy friends in tow, he walked across the silt that passed for the beach area, up the moldy steps and along the pier that disappeared into the pond. He didn't stop at the end of the pier and dove into the water straight as a dropping knife. He rose to the top and swam to the small float where the prettiest and most popular girls always sunbathed, on display like lawn art. He popped himself up onto the float and smirked, flicking droplets from his fingers at the girls who moaned in fake protest. She couldn't hear their voices but she knew the dialogue. She dug her heels into the sand, turned away and went back to her magazine. He's just like all the others – more handsome – but the same, she thought.

She lay motionless, her head inside a borrowed magazine. She read about Elvis and Ricky Nelson, Ava Gardner and Rock Hudson. She peered once or twice over the top of the page and saw him still standing on the float and talking. She tried to disappear into the magazine but found herself distracted and set her gaze on him from time to time. For a moment she thought she saw him looking at her, but thought better of it. Why would he be looking at her? She watched him enter the water again, swim with smooth clean strokes across the pond then shake the water from his hair and ears when he emerged in the shallows. She hoped she was wrong and that he hadn't been looking at her. But she had an uncomfortable feeling inside and the buzzing voice in her head told her. Turning on her side to face away from him as he walked toward her, she pulled a cigarette from the pack of Salems she had taken from her mother's closet and lit it.

"Can I bum one?" he said.

She pulled another from the pack and handed it to him, her hands shaking slightly.

"And a light?" he said.

Without asking, he sat down beside her. She could smell the sun on his skin. His confidence separated him from the boys she knew and she felt out of her depth and a little dizzy. She was used to boys and adults but had no map for this new terrain and felt all the childishness her sixteen years still contained.

"I know who you are. My brother is in one of your classes. You know my brother James," he said.

"You're Rick."

"Yeah, and you're Claire."

"Yeah."

"So what are you doing here?"

"I'm just here. Everybody is here."

"Right. I guess everybody *is* here."

She scanned the pond, saw that the others were watching them and a strange thrill ran through her. He was sitting on her blanket. He was talking with her. She suddenly thought of her father and the whiskey on his breath, then pushed those things from her mind. She had learned how to push things from her mind from an early age. She scanned the pond again, half listening as he talked. He was telling a story about the Philippines and following someone called Huk into the woods. The girls on the float yelled, waving their slim arms in the air for him to come back to them, but he didn't seem to notice. She blushed slightly when she noticed him taking her in as he talked. It wasn't an unpleasant blushing. It was nice, she thought.

Later that night, she lay awkwardly underneath him on a scratchy wool military blanket he had pulled from the trunk of his car. It smelled not vaguely of beach and gasoline. She didn't see metaphorical stars and she didn't blush. Instead she stared dull-eyed and confused out into the infinite past and possible future and at the blinking stars in the black sky far above them as he did what he did.

"Is it cramps, dear?" the school nurse asked.

"Mmmm..." She shook her head yes.

She was both surprised and not surprised when the doctor told her. Her mother was with her that day, smoking a cigarette and silently tapping her shoe in the doorway of the examination room as the news was announced. Sensing her mother's impatience and thinly disguised disgust at the prospect, the doctor had cut to the chase and erased any element of celebration from the proceedings. He announced flatly, "Yes, you are pregnant and I would say eight to nine weeks, which puts your due date at roughly the beginning of March."

Her mother responded with a "pshhhh..." and a cloud of Salem menthol.

At school, arrangements were made quickly as they always were in these cases, and she moved from regular classes to night school where the offense wouldn't contaminate the minds of closed-legged girls who read magazines and dreamed of boys without tattoos and boys who could sing. Girlfriends disappeared. There were no more afterschool phone calls to talk about this disaster or that. There were no more afternoons sipping colas, or girlfriends' compliments and false modesty.

"Oh, this? It was on sale at Seigel's. It's nothing."

There were whispers, averted eyes, and a dull

and distant rumble in her ears where before she'd
heard nothing. Clothing and television, homework,
rides in cars, the sweet thrill of verdant independence
vanished like steam from a summer morning's dewy
grass. Everything changed and then again. The few
remaining friends spoke in tones that told her what
she had done. They kept their questions and their
pity was matched only by the secret thrill they felt to
be so close to the act. In fact, they took some
proprietorship in the act in their gossip and
luxuriated in the glow of being so close to the shame.
They thanked god it wasn't them.

At home, her mother drank and blew smoke.
Her father, usually cruel and oppressive, retreated
from her. At least there was this. She felt a strange
power inside her that she didn't understand
completely and her condition put her father on his
back foot somehow. All that bullying stopped in its
tracks by a baby, she marveled to herself. When the
Marine asked for permission to marry her, her father
played the role and gave his approval. As if the script
wasn't written, as if they didn't all know their roles.
They could have all saved the trouble of the acting –
simply said, "this" – all signed their names and called
it a life.

She slept in the same small bed with the same

embroidered blanket. Tiny ballerinas danced with perfect form across her sleep, which was both fitful and filled with worry. Vivid dreams raced across her mind from a strange place. She had the sensation that she only saw a piece of the dream and that there was much more dreaming outside the farthest edge – but she couldn't see quite far enough. It was like arriving late to a movie and leaving early – which she also did, depending on her nausea. She saw *That Touch Of Mink* and *The Music Man*, both of which she found foolish. The air in the movie theatre was thick with breath and butter and sugar which was not pleasing, but to sit alone in the dark during the bright afternoon was good. Just to sit in the dark, alone, was a balm to her. On several afternoons she found her seat without knowing which film she had purchased a ticket to. She hadn't bought a ticket to a film – she had bought a ticket to the gentle darkness of the theatre itself and the heavy sweet air inside.

There were dates with the Marine that weren't really dates. There were vague plans made and decisions that needed deciding so they were decided. This place or that? This thing or that thing? She didn't care either way but found it easier to voice an opinion than to endure the endless discussion. An apartment, dishes or a brand of cigarettes – all seemed to her to be the same magnitude of decision. She wasn't sure if that made the apartment unimportant or the cigarettes very important. She only knew she cared about the same either way.

When the small day before the big day came, she found herself draped in a scratchy white dress, her belly protesting at the seams and confirming what remaining rumors were still unconfirmed. She was nauseous and dizzy. There were tears from aunts who loved her and knew. There were jokes about the color of her dress from drunk and loud uncles. From her mother, there was menthol smoke blown at the fluorescent lights hanging from the ceiling in their white metal cowlings. Forty or so guests drank ginger ale, ate egg sandwiches, spilled coffee and gossiped like pigeons in the metal folding chairs. Men did their best with the free beer and the women thought of how things should be and how things could be. Some of them pretended that things just are and isn't it wonderful? Isn't it just wonderful?

After the guests, her mother, his mother, and her friends were gone, she picked up the paper cups and the napkins mouthed with smudges of cake. She emptied the glass ashtrays that said "Moose Lodge 3452 Dover New Hampshire" into the garbage pail and washed them with hot soapy water in the big industrial steel sink. She pushed the broom slowly across the green and white linoleum tile until the dust and scraps were in a neat pile then, lacking a dustpan, borrowed a magazine from the lobby to brush the pile onto. She emptied the dirt from Ricky Nelson's glossy black and white face and returned the magazine. Then she piled the chairs back into the storage closet one by one, shut out the fluorescent lights, closed the door behind her and stepped out into the icy January darkness. He was leaning against the Chevy, laughing, with two red-faced friends, and slightly drunk. She felt a small kick inside her.

The car really was a curious color, she thought. It's hard to tell in the dull light of dusk if it's salmon colored or if that's a fancy way of saying pink – to sell you something you don't know if you really want. In time she would know. In time she understood how many things in life are salmon colored.

Bottom of the Well

Eric sat splayed across the pull-out sofa as wide as his limbs could spread. Program listings from the satellite service scrolled the large, cheap, flat screen television mounted to the wall in front of him. An endless loop rolled as Eric's thumb pressed the remote. On the Goodwill table beside the sofa, a tall glass of vodka with ice was sweating slightly and adding to the geography of water stains on the table-top. In the corner sat a suitcase that had been opened once and left opened since Eric had arrived. The clothes in the suitcase were barely arranged, the book in the suitcase un-cracked. Only the toothbrush showed any sign of use.

In the two weeks previous to his arrival at his parents' small farmhouse in Brownville, Maine, Eric had been fired from his job at a prestigious Ivy League school, arrested for domestic assault, and spent six days in a county jail. He was now living out of a very expensive suitcase on the porch of his parents' house. His only trip into town since he'd arrived had been to the grocery store to stock up on vodka.

Upstairs, in a very small attic room, Eric's mother Brenda chain-smoked hand-rolled menthol cigarettes and knitted. Her tiny television set glowed twenty-four hours a day – usually news programs, but also "Dancing with the Stars" and true crime re-enactments. On the other side of the wall where the giant porch television scrolled, Eric's father's bedroom was decorated with a range of hunting motifs – cheap paintings of Labrador Retrievers with ducks in their soft mouths, proud deer with enormous antlers standing beside tall pines, and a black bear clawing a fish from a running stream. A gun rack was mounted on the outside wall and cradled a Mossberg 12-gauge double barrel, an Ithica 20-gauge single barrel, an ancient Winchester thirty-ought-six and a Wetherby 308.

Eric took a long swallow from the glass. Tony, Eric's father, rapped his knuckles on the porch door but did not wait for an answer before walking in.

"What you watching?"

"I'm not."

"What you gonna be watching?"

"I'm not."

"You wanna go into town with me? I need to fill the K-2 tank and your mother needs some stuff for her stew."

"No. Thanks."

"Might be good for you. Just to move around?"

"This is good for me."

"Okay. You need anything while I'm down there?"

"Nope."

"Okay, I'll leave you to it then."

Tony walked outside, his breath a fog in the cold, and started the truck. He sat still in the cabin until he saw the temperature gauge give slightly, then drove off.

Eric's thumb continued its endless search. He was thinking about the jail. He wondered what his sentence would be, though it seemed somehow impossible to him that he would go back. He had two long months to wait until his hearing and the thought that he would be sitting there on the sofa-bed, endlessly scrolling the satellite listings until his court date, filled him with a dread as dark as the thought of jail itself. He took another long swallow of cold vodka and closed his eyes. His medications mixed with the alcohol in a not unpleasant haze. He could feel the blackness in his head, and yet he could also let the blackness simply sit there.

Brenda knocked lightly on the porch door. Eric did not answer. Brenda knocked again.

"Yes?"

"Sweetheart, do you want something to eat?"

"No. I'm fine."

"But you haven't eaten hardly at all. Don't you think you should eat?"

"No. I'm fine."

"Are you sure you don't want anything?"

"Yes. I'm fine."

"Yes you would like something?"

"No. Yes, I'm sure I'm fine and that I don't want anything."

"Okay. But you let me know. I can make you something real nice."

Eric opened his eyes and said sharply, "I'm fine."

Outside, the sky drenched the snowfall with the deepest blue. *The bluest sky of the day.* Eric thought of the photographer he had dated long ago who had explained the blue-hour to him. The woman had been a talented photographer and Eric recalled her description of how photographers revered those few short minutes between light and dark when the sky was its deepest, bluest shade. She'd made it sound almost mystical and he remembered her genuine awe and excitement in sharing it with him when she had taken him outside the bar they'd been in to look into the sky. He'd felt a kind of unnerved feeling that in all his life he had never noticed the phenomenon before. Her sharing it with him had made him feel unsophisticated. Now he stared out the window into its depth, the barely visible outline of a crow on a telephone wire the only movement outside.

When he'd been let go from his position at Yale, it had been without dramatics. The department head had been monitoring Eric's comings and goings and had kept tidy notes on Eric's increasing drinking problem and its effect on the department. There had been many missed meetings, missed deadlines, missed details and in the last few weeks almost no actual work done, so that when the head had called Eric in, there was little for him to say or do but push the notes across the table and tell Eric he was being let go. He'd been fired on a Friday, of course, so there were just a few hours to gather his things, turn in his credentials and leave for the day, as he would on any Friday.

Eric had even felt some small satisfaction that the charade was over. In his last hour at Yale he sat, feet on his desk, leaning far back in the expensive office chair, and drinking the rest of the vodka he had secreted away in the locked bottom drawer of his desk. He watched YouTube videos of Iggy Pop and

Lou Reed on the computer while he drank. When he left his office he simply dropped the empty bottle in the trash container and walked out. He left the computer on with hours of videos queued to play – his final protest.

Eric lifted his thumb from the remote control. The receiver landed on a game show. He pressed his thumb again, then let it off. The receiver landed on a news program. Eric thought to himself that he'd invented a game, and that there must be some way to wager on what program the receiver would land on. He'd work it out later. For a moment, a panic grabbed at him as he wondered how much vodka he had left and thought he might call his father and reach him while he was still at the grocery. He reached between the sofa cushions and found his phone. Then he remembered the other fifth he'd hidden in the barn when he'd arrived, and relief swept over him. He drained his glass.

Eric did not fully remember attacking his wife. She'd woken him from a deep, drunk, slumber to request an errand of him, and he'd simply attacked her without notice. Later it turned out that she had filmed the episode with her phone camera. This simple fact – that she had known he might assault her – was mortifying to Eric. The fact of the assault was difficult enough, but that he'd been set up to react like a teased dog or a spoiled child horrified him as much as the photographs of the deep bruises on his wife's neck. There was also a photograph that showed her reddened jaw, where he'd first struck her. By the time the police had taken him away and were booking him, Eric had sobered enough to understand what was happening. In the wired glass of the holding cell he had caught a glimpse of himself grinning strangely, wild-eyed like a trapped animal.

Eric heard the sound of tires crunching in the frozen snow outside as Tony's truck pulled slowly up the steep grade in four-wheel drive. The front steps rumbled with his father's indelicate entrance and the door banged shut, shaking the walls of the old farm house slightly. Through the porch door, he could hear his father whistling to himself as he put the groceries away. Knuckles rapped on the door and it opened again.

"Still looking for something to watch?"

"Not really."

"There's movies on that Lifetime network."

"Yeah, I'll find something."

"Them stories are real on that Lifetime network."

"I'm fine. Don't worry about me."

"Well. I'm just trying to make you comfortable."

"You're letting all the cold in."

Tony stepped onto the porch and closed the door loudly behind him.

"So have you talked to a lawyer?"

"Yeah."

"So what did he say?"

"Not much."

"Did he say when you're gonna know something?"

"I've told you a hundred times."

"Told me what?"

"I've told you a hundred times, I won't know anything until the hearing."

"Oh. I just thought maybe you talked to a lawyer again. I ain't trying to bug you. This is hard for your mother, you know. She's real upset."

"Yeah, I realize that. She's not the one who has to go through it, though."

"Well. I'm just asking. Trying to make her feel a little bit better, you know? Trying to calm her down."

"Tell her to try this," Eric held up the empty glass.

"That's what got you living on a porch."

Tony walked back into the house. Eric pressed his thumb to the remote. QVC. Eric closed his eyes and listened as two women talked excitedly about a cubic zirconium ring. An hour later, knuckles rapped, then the door opened again.

"Your mother made beef stew."

"I'm not hungry."

"Can't you just have some, you know, for her? It'll make her feel better."

"Okay, okay…"

Eric went into the kitchen where the tiny woman was stooped over a huge pot. The enormous farm table was set for three.

"Now I made this just for you, 'cause I know it's your favorite."

"Thanks."

"So sit down and we're gonna fix you all up."

"I'm sitting."

The old woman dished out an enormous bowl of stew and set it in front of Eric.

"I can't eat this much."

"Well, just do what you can."

"Your mother makes the best stew."

"Have you heard anything from the lawyer?"

"I just told dad – no. I keep telling you I won't know anything until the hearing. Why do I have to keep telling you the same damn thing over and over?"

"Well, I was just asking. I thought maybe you talked to him again, that's all. Shouldn't you stay on top of it? Shouldn't you be going to meetings?"

Eric picked up his bowl and walked back out onto the porch and slammed the door shut. He set the bowl down on the Goodwill table, then returned to his position on the sofa with the remote control. Thumb down: game show. Thumb down: King Kong remake.

Outside the wind began to blow. Eric could feel the cold slipping past the windows and across his arms. He took a spoonful of the stew. It was good but he wasn't hungry, so he pushed the bowl away. Through the wall he heard muffled voices and the sound of dishes and pots and pans being washed, dried, and put away. The darkness in his head was an all-consuming self-loathing. Eric closed his eyes and tried to quiet the black humming, but his thoughts only raced faster, the darkness only filled his head more fully. He thought about his lover, now un-tethered from him, sitting alone in her house. She would have heard by now, he felt sure, but he didn't have the strength to text or call her. He was empty — empty of empathy, empty of sadness, empty even of his usual false confidence that announced itself with his anger. He felt nothing but a great black void where his mind should be and a hole inside begging to be filled with alcohol. He was even past the point of shame. He felt nothing but the begging emptiness.

In the kitchen, Tony washed the dishes and Brenda sat. Her head hung, and small thin tears ran down her wrinkled and hollow cheeks.

"It's hard to believe all this."

"I know, Brenda. There's nothing we can do."

"It's just hard to believe. I don't know why he won't do something."

"There's nothing we can do."

"There must be something. Do you think we should try to call Traci? Maybe see if she'll drop the charges?"

"It don't work that way, Brenda. It ain't her filed the charges. These things is different these days. It's the police that files the charges. I don't think she even has much say in it."

"I just don't understand." Then came a racking sob.

"C'mon, dear. I'll get you back upstairs. I'll try to talk to him again tomorrow."

"I just can't imagine all this. It doesn't seem real."

Tony lifted her arm and when she stood he pulled her close to him and held her. He took her elbow and walked her up the steep steps to the attic bedroom. Brenda sat on her bed, buried her face in her hands and began to sob.

"Which ones of these pills is your night-time ones?"

"I'll get them," she sniffed.

"Just tell me which ones and I'll bring them to you."

"Bring them all, and my magnifying glass."

Tony scooped up the stand of bottles, placed them in her lap, then brought her enormous magnifying glass and sat beside her helping her open the bottles as she inspected the labels and picked out the correct pills.

"Christ, that's a lot of pills. You sure about which ones?"

"Yes." Brenda sniffed.

"I'll get you some juice."

"Half water, half juice, honey."

"Okay. I'll be right back."

Tony returned with the juice, and Brenda took the palm full of pills one at a time, each with a small sip. Tony counted to nine. He sat beside her.

"I'll talk to him tomorrow. Maybe I can get him to go to a meeting in Milo."

"He won't go. He won't do anything."

"We'll see. I'll talk to him again.

"What do you think the sentence will be?"

"I have no idea."

"Ed said it would be between three months and a year."

"Well, I could do three months standing on my head," Tony tried.

"I still can't imagine all this. He'll never recover from this."

"He can. It's up to him. He's just not ready yet, I guess…"

"I guess. I just can't imagine all this."

The television flickered in the dim room, throwing colors around the walls. Tony grabbed two cigarettes from a wicker basket on the nightstand and handed one to Brenda. She reached into the deep pocket of her fluffy bathrobe to retrieve the lighter, then lit her cigarette, and Tony's as well. Her crying stopped. They both sat on the edge of her bed inhaling deeply and blowing the smoke in the direction of a tiny fan that sat balanced on the sill of the window opened just a crack. When he finished his cigarette Tony stood, wobbling.

"I'll go shut everything down and put one more wood in the fire. I love you."

"I love you too..." Brenda reached for another cigarette.

When she heard Tony's steps at the bottom of the stairwell, she reached under her bed and pulled out a bottle of cheap vodka. She filled her juice glass to the top and returned the bottle under the bed. She took a long deep swallow and stared at the television, blowing smoke at the fan. Her eyes were already glazed from the medications.

On the porch, Eric slipped on his boots. They were the wrong boots for this snow, but he had only been allowed into the house for ten minutes to retrieve things while the officer waited, so he had taken what he found first for clothing and concentrated on getting his computer, checkbook and financial pieces. Now he slipped on his jacket and went out into the blackness. A sliver of moon gave him just enough light to find his way to the shed and he quickly grabbed the bottle from under the workbench and scurried shivering back to the porch. Through the wall, he heard his father creaking down the cellar stairs to put another log in the woodstove.

Eric twisted the plastic cap until it snapped loose. He took a small sip from the cold vodka. It had no taste to him anymore, but he felt its strong vapor in his nose and his mind un-tightened slightly at the sensation. He waited until he heard his father come back up the stairs, and close his own bedroom door and then he slipped from the porch into the house and filled his glass with ice, being careful to make as little sound as possible. As he went back onto the porch, he saw the flicker of his father's television from under the bedroom door and heard his father's light snoring already. Eric filled his glass and sat back into the pull-out sofa. He scanned the listings, found nothing again, and set the television to CNN with the sound turned very low. He drank late into the evening, the vodka dancing with the painkillers in a slow waltz that eventually found its way to sleep.

In the morning, Tony was awake very early and though he made no effort to be quiet, Eric did not stir. Outside it was already the golden hour – the other time of day photographers revered – when the sun was low and the light the most red it would be all day, splashing rich and deep gold light across the world. The blue hour would follow soon enough. In the late morning, Tony opened the porch door to find Eric splayed out on the sofa-bed, sleeping deeply. It wasn't until late afternoon that Tony heard some fumbling from the porch. He decided to give Eric time to fully wake before speaking with him.

Upstairs in her tiny attic room, Brenda had been awake for many hours but had not stirred much aside from the steady blow of cigarette smoke into the nicotine yellowed fan. Things in the farmhouse ran on their own peculiar clock. Tony brought Brenda her breakfast in the afternoon – always the same – one egg over-hard on a piece of buttered wheat toast. A few hours later, Brenda shuffled downstairs to cook dinner for Tony. Sometimes she ate. Sometimes she didn't, though she always sat with him.

"Have you talked to him today?"

"No, he just now got up. Here's your egg. You make sure you eat it now, okay? The whole thing."

"Just now he got up?"

"I think so. I looked in earlier but he was sleeping."

Brenda took her small plate with the egg and the fork and set it in her lap.

"You eat that whole thing. It's good for you."

"I will."

"Maybe I should call Traci? Do you think I should call her?

"No. I don't. It wouldn't make any difference and you don't want to make things worse. We just have to wait. That's all we can do."

"Well, it's killing me. All this, it's killing me."

"I know but there's nothing to be done. I can't get him to go anywhere, do anything. I can't force him. There's nothing to be done. We have to wait. You eat that."

As the golden hour slowly gave way to the blue hour, Eric decided how to gamble with the remote control. He palmed several painkillers and swallowed them with the last of his vodka. Then he pushed his thumb down on the remote control and held it for a very long time. He closed his eyes then took his thumb from the remote. He opened his eyes. Game show.

He snuck from the porch into the house. He heard his parents' faint voices from the attic stairwell. He went to his father's bedroom, took the 12-gauge from its rest, dropped shells into both barrels, and walked out into the snow. He was not wearing a coat but did not feel the cold. Above him the deepest, most beautiful blue he had ever seen blanketed the sky.

Falling Down

When they found her, she was at impossible angles. And so they knew right away. One of her shoes was missing. There was a red ribbon tied in her hair and Ed thought it curious that the ribbon could still be tied there – like the last leaf on a tree after a hurricane. She was a small woman and looked like a large doll tossed from the window of a passing car into the bushes, near the railroad tracks. None of them recognized her, which would have been difficult anyway. At first, they did not move her. They called the photographer from the coroner's office to attend to his job of shooting the scene. They walked carefully around the body looking for anything that might help account for her display. Officer Ed Stoppard was troubled by the missing shoe and ranged farther from her than he knew he needed to, frustrated that he could not find it. A wind blew through the trees; the leaves of a poplar – looked like spinning coins in its wake.

"Were there any missing persons last night?" asked Ed.

"Nothing I can see from the log."

"What about for the whole week?"

"She's only been here overnight."

"I can see that, but she might have gotten herself into something a few days back."

The flash of the photographer's camera disrupted the men and they gathered back near the cruiser to let him do his job. It was early evening and the sun had dropped below the tree line. The photographer was chasing the day's light.

*

The night before, Deborah had started the late shift at the Lakeside Bar at nine o'clock and she'd been a few minutes late. Her boss, Jerry Fernald, admonished her in a teasing way. Deborah was always late. Everyone knew Deborah was always late.

"You decided to show up after all."

"I'm sorry Jerry. I just lost track."

"You're gonna lose a job if you keep losing track."

"Oh yeah? Who else would put up with you?"

"I'll think on that."

The old man always teased Deborah in an easy way like that.

*

After the photographs were taken, Ed walked back to the body. He carefully pulled at her clothing to see if he could locate any I.D. in any pockets. There was nothing.

"Could have been an accident. She might have just got hit and thrown back here."

"No, she was put here," said Ed.

"How do you know that already?"

"Because she's too far back from the road. She wouldn't be this far back in here and there's nothing in the grass from any direction. She was dumped right here. From a car."

Ed looked around one last time in the fading light, his heavy black flashlight held high in his right hand to illuminate as much ground as possible. Then the men from the coroner's office took the body and drove away. The other officers filled out preliminary reports as Ed wandered through the tall weeds where she'd been found. *Where was her other shoe?* He kept wondering.

*

When the men had asked her if she wanted to party, Deborah initially refused. The kids were home, with her mother babysitting, and she didn't want to be out any later than she needed. But then she remembered that her mother had said she would stay over, which she sometimes did since Deborah's shift didn't end until one AM. The two men seemed decent enough, they weren't being pushy and they had a bit of blow with them. She couldn't resist a nice line or two. And so after she closed the bar up for the night she met them in the parking lot, and instead of going home she drove off with them in their red Firebird. They drove to a secluded picnic area out at the edge of town, shared a bottle of Canadian Club and snorted a few lines, all three of them chain smoking cigarettes. The coke was not great stuff but they laughed and partied.

*

The next morning Ed sat sipping coffee at his desk at the police station in Brunswick, Maine. Brunswick was a small town and so this kind of crime was unusual – not unheard of, but unusual. The few murders that Ed had worked over his twenty years on the force had been simple enough. It was always the husband, the jealous boyfriend or the jilted lover. He'd never struggled to figure out who was responsible in the past and figured this one to be the same. He thought about his own ex-wife and thought maybe both of them had made it through their divorce by the skin of their teeth. There were a couple weeks when it could have been either one of them. He wondered about the missing shoe again and it bothered him.

"We got a name from last night."

"What we got?" asked Ed

"Deborah Adams. Thirty-four. Divorced. Worked at the Lakeside."

"I'll go over this morning. Anything else?"

"Nope. Her mother called in this morning. Early. Said she didn't come home from her shift. ID-ed her this morning first thing. Three kids."

"Shit."

"No shit. The kids are with the mother."

Ed drove the few miles down the two-lane highway out towards the lake. The sun was high when he arrived, and though it was cool enough, the bright sun glaring through the car's windows had broken a sweat under his arms, turning the dark blue shirt a darker blue. Ed knocked his firm cop-knock on the office door and Jerry opened it and told him to come inside.

Ed could see the old man's eyes were red and swollen. There was whiskey on his breath.

"So you heard?"

"Yeah. I heard. She was a good kid, you know. She wasn't like people thought. She was late all the time and yeah, she partied a little bit, but she was a good kid. I don't know what her little ones are gonna do."

"They're with her mom right now. You got any ideas about who this might be? Anything stick out from last night?"

"No, I left early last night, Ed. I usually do on Wednesdays cause it gets slow earlier, you know. Deborah's locked up plenty of times, never had any trouble before. This ain't that kind of place out here. We don't have too much rough stuff, you know?"

"I know Jerry, but you do now. I'm right in thinking you got no cameras?"

"No, we don't got cameras." The old man's eyes watered and he rubbed them with the back of his hand.

"You got anything for me, Jerry? Was she seeing anyone? Boyfriend? Lover?"

"Nope. Long as she's been working for me, I never seen Deborah with anyone. She'd have a drink here after her shift, if she was the early shift, but I don't know her to be with any men. She seemed soured on 'em on account of her divorce was hard, she said."

"Where is he?"

"Never seen him. She said he moved down Florida after she got custody. Said he was a real bastard."

"They're graded on a curve. She's met a real bastard now, if he wasn't one."

*

When they had finished the bottle of whiskey and the small folded paper square of coke, Deborah checked her watch. It was nearly four in the morning and she felt a small sadness inside in spite of her racing heart.

"I should be getting back soon. You think you can bring me back to my car now?"

"But you said you wanted to party?"

"Yeah, this was awesome. You guys are fun but I should get back. My mom is watching the kids."

Neither of the men answered her. They glanced at each other. Her heart sank as she thought of her children.

*

Back where she'd been found, Ed toed through the tall weeds again. He saw the flattened grass where she'd lain and where the dried black blood that had trickled from her mouth and nose had pooled on the sandy ground. Tall weeds touched his hands as he walked in widening concentric circles around the flattened patch of grass and blood. He walked slowly and deliberately, looking carefully for something, anything at all, they might have missed the night before. But he found nothing. Where was that god-damn shoe? Ed drove back to the station.

"Did you get anything from old Jerry?"

"Not much. He left early last night and let her close."

"Nothing else from the mother either. No boyfriends?"

"Doesn't look like it. Jerry was pretty upset and it sounded like he knew her pretty well."

"Anything about him?"

"No, no, no. That old man is feeble as a two-legged stool. He's really broken up. He had no hand in this. We get a report from the coroner?"

"Yup, just now. Strangled."

"Well, hell, we saw that. Anything they can tell us about it?"

"He didn't use anything. He used his hands."

"Okay. I'll go over there later. We don't have much, do we?"

"I'd say that's true. We don't have much at all."

*

The Firebird drove out of the picnic area with its headlights off until it reached the main road. The driver looked carefully down both long stretches east and west before pulling onto the main road, then pulled the headlamp knob on. In the east, the sun was just beginning its steep climb; a hint of blue morning cracked the horizon line, the rest of the black sky still dizzy with stars.

*

Ed lay in bed. Beside him a short whiskey sat on the nightstand. He stared at the ceiling, unable to sleep. From the bedroom window, an air conditioner hummed to him. He turned the television on, walked the remote through the channels, then shut it back off again. Ed knew by now he was long gone, whoever it was, and it angered him. He lay in bed for hours not sleeping, unable to wipe the image of her small crumpled frame from his mind. Eventually, a troubled sleep found him. In a cheap hotel room on the Vermont – New Hampshire border, one hundred miles away from Ed's troubled sleep, two drunk men argued.

"We was both there."

"I never touched her."

"You sat and watched."

"I didn't touch her."

"Don't make no difference. You was there and so was I. It just got a little out of control and that's all. It didn't have to end up like that."

"It sure looked like you intended it to."

"And what did you do about it? Watched like a TV show."

"Fuck you."

"No. Fuck you."

Someone banged hard on the wall of their room. The two men, suddenly aware of their loud drunk voices stopped. One of the men grabbed the remote control from the nightstand between the two beds and turned the television on.

"Quit changing it so fast," the other said.

*

Ed woke and made coffee. It was his day off, but he couldn't settle into it with what was running around his head, so he dressed and went to the station. He looked through the reports again, waiting for the Lakeside to open, then drove back over to the bar. He found the old man in the cramped back office looking unkempt and unwashed. Dark circles ringed his red eyes. Ed thought the old man looked like he'd aged another five years overnight.

"There has to be something, Jerry. She didn't leave in her car. We found her all the way over near Deerfield at the tracks. She left here with somebody that she didn't expect to leave with. Otherwise, she would have been dropped off, but she drove here. Her mother was watching her kids; she drove to work in her own car. She must have expected to leave in her own car, but she didn't. She left with someone from here, someone that was here that night. There has to be something, goddamn it, Jerry."

"Ed, we get all sorts out here. Being by the lake, we get campers, hunters, people from the city. Yeah, we got regulars, but we get people from all over coming through here."

"Can you remember which of your regulars were here Wednesday night, Jerry?"

"Probably. Let me talk to Donnie and see if we can remember exactly. He was bar-back that night."

"Okay. Make a list for me and I'll be back for it this afternoon."

Ed drove the cruiser back to the station. He looked up Deborah's address and drove toward the house. He pulled the car over at the corner of a cross street near the home and sat. He saw in the yard a few brightly colored children's toys and a small swing-set. A small mutt lay sleeping on the rotting porch. He wondered if her mother would eventually come for the dog.

*

The next morning the two hungover men woke groggy to the sound of the hotel's cleaners knocking on their door. They were slow to respond and so the cleaner opened the door and walked in, then apologized in a thick accent and backed out of the

room to their half-awake protest. Deborah's leather
purse sat on the nightstand, plastic cups filled with
whiskey-soaked cigarette butts on either side. The
television flickered. The two men sat on the edges of
the two beds trying to bring the awake world to
them. One of them lit a cigarette and tossed the pack
and lighter across the space between them. The other
caught them then looked at the purse.

"What the fuck?"

"What?"

"I thought you tossed it?"

"It's leather, you idiot. It's worth something."

"Fucking shit you are stupid. We can't be
driving around with her stuff."

"We'll sell it at a pawn shop. Probably get
twenty bucks for it."

"Fucking shit. You are so fucking stupid."

"Then I'll keep the twenty bucks. Fuck you."

*

Again that night Ed slept restlessly. Time was
passing quickly and he had nothing to follow. When
he woke, he made coffee. He looked at his face in
the bathroom mirror and saw dark lines under his
red eyes that reminded him of Jerry. He stared into

the mirror at his own visage, thinking about the swing-set, the dog sleeping on the porch, and again wondered about the shoe. There had to be something he could follow, but he couldn't find what it might be. He drove to the station, checked in to see if anything had been reported overnight, then sat at his desk thinking. He decided he would get the list of regulars from Jerry and speak with them. As it was still early, he called Jerry at his home, and wrote down their names, recognizing a few as he scribbled. Then he started calling them. He spoke with several who remembered nothing then spoke to a man, Pete Hawley, who worked at one of the two auto body shops in town.

"Pete, this is Ed from the police department."

A rough hung-over voice answered. "I figured it wasn't good."

"It's nothing about you, Pete. I'm calling about last Wednesday."

"I was at the Lakeside, but I didn't see anything, Ed. I wish I could help."

"What time did you leave?"

"Just before closing."

"Do you remember who was there still when you left?"

"There were a few stragglers. Jimmy from the dock was there still I think."

"Did you see anything odd at all when you left? Anything at all."

"Nope. Nothing. She was a good girl, Ed. She never gave anyone any problem. She partied a bit but, you know, she was just a regular girl."

"What about in the parking lot?"

"I thought you wanted to know who was there?"

"Anything at all, Pete."

"Well, the only thing I can think of was there was a red Firebird in the lot. I thought that was a little funny. Someone at the lake in a Firebird. You know? That's not a car you go camping in."

"Did you see the plate?"

"No, but it was out of state. I remember that because that's what made me think it was funny – someone driving from out of state in a Firebird to go camping. Lousy Bondo job on it too. Surprised they didn't have to get towed out. It's still really wet back in there."

Ed added the Firebird to the BOLO and resent it to the region. Maybe it was something. Maybe it was nothing. He drove back to where the body had been found, parked the cruiser and sat thinking.

*

At the hotel room the two men dressed, then tidied the room. On their way out one of the men saw a sign on the door – Strictly No Smoking, it said. One of them went back in and grabbed the trash bag with the cups of cigarette butts sitting at the top and brought it to a trash container outside. They left the hotel room door wide open, hoping the room would air out. One of them put the purse in the trunk of the car. Then they got into the red Firebird and drove across the street to a diner. They ordered the special and sat waiting for their order. A few minutes later a man of dark complexion walked into the diner and to their table.

"You must not smoke in the rooms," he said.

"We didn't smoke in your room."

"You smoked. There is a charge for the extra cleaning for smoking in the room."

"You must be thinking about another room. We didn't smoke in your room, buddy."

"Yes, you did. You need to pay the cleaning fee. Room 203."

"Listen, we didn't smoke in your room."

"You smoked. Our cleaner saw the cigarettes and the room stinks of smoke. You will pay for the cleaning."

"Hold on, how much is the cleaning?" the other man said.

"Three hundred dollars."

"Buddy, you're out of your mind. We didn't smoke in there. We don't even smoke." A pack of cigarettes bulged from his t-shirt pocket.

The hotel manager pointed at his shirt pocket.

"Look we don't want any trouble. How much will you take? We don't have three hundred dollars."

The other diners watched as the argument escalated and voices raised.

"Three hundred dollars is what I'll take. You signed the paper when you checked in."

"We paid cash. You got the wrong room, buddy." The two men had stopped eating their breakfast.

The owner of the diner walked to the table.

"Is there a problem here?"

"These men smoked in the room and need to pay the cleaning fee."

"Let's take it outside if we're gonna keep this up. I got customers here," the owner said.

"Let me see how much we have, okay?" one of them said.

"You better have three hundred dollars," the hotel man said.

The diners watched nervously as the two rough men got up and all four of them walked outside.

The two men pulled their wallets and counted out eighty dollars.

"Another two hundred twenty dollars please. Everything will need to be cleaned. The carpet, the drapes, everything."

"Hold on. Just relax. Let me look. You stay here," he said to the other man. He reached into his pocket of his dirty jeans, fished the keys then went to the Firebird and opened the trunk. The other man nodded, then pulled a cigarette and lit it, his hands shaking.

*

Ed walked the perimeter of the scene as he'd done the day before. He kept thinking about the missing shoe. As he already knew he would, he found nothing, then drove back to the police station. As he pulled into the parking lot, the radio crackled to life.

*

The man leaned over into the trunk of the car to hide his movements and emptied the purse contents onto the floor of the trunk. He gathered what money there was and turned and closed the trunk. The cleaning woman who had opened the door earlier crossed the street to the diner.

"I got another hundred bucks here, buddy. Can we call it even?"

"Three hundred dollars is the cleaning fee."

"This is all we got. We don't want any trouble."

Inside the hotel office, the owner's wife watched nervously from the window and dialed the telephone. A few minutes later, as the men continued to argue, a police cruiser pulled into the dusty gravel lot.

"These men smoked in the room," the hotel manager said.

The two men looked at each other.

"They must pay the cleaning fee."

"Honestly, officer, this is all we have."

"Can I see some I.D.?"

Both men pulled their wallets out and handed their licenses to the officer.

The police radio crackled inside the car but the officer, busied for the moment ignored it.

*

Ed listened to the radio as it updated the BOLO with his new information about the red Firebird, then went into his office. He felt foolish about it but added one more thing to the BOLO – the missing shoe.

*

At the diner, the officer took the two licenses and got into his cruiser. He ran the license numbers, found nothing and as he opened the car door the radio sparked to life. Over the static, he heard something about a Firebird and a shoe but thought to himself that it was from way over in Maine. Nothing to do with this car or these men. He thought he might be able to get the hotel owner to accept the one hundred and eighty dollars so that he would not have to spend the morning writing out a report for something so trivial.

"That's a lousy Bondo job," the man from the diner said under his breath.

The smoking man glared at him.

"Well, I can see all the sanding marks," he said louder.

"Make them look in their purse," said the chambermaid.

"What?" said the officer

"They have a purse. Make them open their purse."

"Hold on now, we ain't got no purse and we're trying to be square here. That's everything we got on us. That's every dime," the smoking man said.

"I'll tell you what. I'll go through the whole car and see if I can find even a dollar more," said the other man.

The officer gave the hotel manager a slightly pleading look.

"Fine. Give me the cash now but I'll go through the car," the hotel man said.

"No. We can't do that, Dinesh. I'll go through the car. Do I have permission to search the car, you two?"

The two men looked at each other and, seeing the thinness of their situation, nodded. The officer opened the car door and efficiently went through the glove box and the console box. He pushed his hands down between the seats and seat backs and pulled out a few coins which he placed on the roof top. He checked the backseat, found two single dollar bills which he handed to the hotel manager, then pushed the lever to move the front seat back and looked under the seats, feeling with his hands. Under the passenger side seat he found a woman's shoe. His hand trembled slightly as he recognized what it was but left it there.

"Okay, that's done now. Just give me a minute and we can be done with this."

The two rough men looked at each other with relief.

"I still say that's a lousy Bondo job," said the diner man, turning to go back inside.

"Yeah, I guess you're right about that. I ain't too good with Bondo," the smoking man replied, then flicked his butt and reached in his shirt pocket for another smoke. Dinesh walked back to the hotel with the cleaning woman; he was deeply disappointed.

The officer went to his car and called in to the station. The Vermont station called Ed. He was sipping a lukewarm coffee at his desk. Ed hit the lights and drove the hundred miles to the diner in Vermont. When he arrived, the two men were handcuffed in the back seat of the cruiser, its flashing blue lights dancing with the flashing blue light of

Ed's own cruiser. The Firebird's trunk was open, displaying the contents of Deborah's empty purse. Three tattered school photos of children lay among the belongings. The officer recounted the story to Ed. They sat together in Ed's cruiser going over details. They moved the two men to the backseat of Ed's cruiser and he drove east. When they reached the Maine state line, Ed pulled the car over, picked up the shoe from the seat next to him and got out of the car. Then he opened the back door and smashed the shoe into the face of one of the men, leaving a bloody gash in the man's upper lip. He went around to the other side and did the same, then wiped the shoe carefully with a cleaning wipe, threw the wipe from his window and continued driving. Back at the station, Ed found that the shoe did not match the one Deborah was wearing the night she was killed. He never did find her other shoe.

Hard Luck Baby

When Marlene started stripping, she was only sixteen but looked a few years older. Everyone told her so. She had the geometry of a grown woman, though within it, of course, the mind of a teenager. She found herself thrilled with the attention. Her home life was dull. Her sullen and alcoholic father watched television from his ratty recliner and drank himself into a stupor most nights. Marlene's mother was a mouse of a woman who feared her husband's sporadic raging, and so she kept herself small in their home. Marlene's older brother, whom she adored, had joined the Army when Marlene was still in elementary school. His leaving had instigated a rebellious streak that began with Marlene inking a small homemade tattoo into her forearm. "Nothing Left To Lose," it said in small crooked blue letters. It was the title of her favorite album by her favorite band. The tattoo was fading already by the time she turned sixteen.

Sometimes she covered the tattoo with foundation makeup she stole from the drug store a few dark streets away from her home in Portsmouth.

She stole often. Sometimes because she wanted a thing, but sometimes just to see if she could, and for the small rush it gave her. Sometimes, after she stole, she liked to loiter around the entrance of the store for a few moments to more fully feel the small rush. Marlene was a beautiful girl who had become hard, and so she attracted the attention of men who liked beautiful and hard girls.

When she stripped, she enjoyed the control she could feel over the grown men. It was a pleasant feeling to have all the eyes on her, to hold court with her beautiful body. She picked her own music for the DJ to play, mostly Aerosmith and AC/DC, which she found easy to dance to. After counting the pile of one and five and ten dollar bills that made up her first night's earnings, Marlene never went back to school. The school never called her parents and her parents never called the school. Her parents never questioned her late nights or her money. They lived separate lives in the same dark house.

Occasionally, a postcard would arrive from her brother. Marlene cherished the postcards and always wrote back immediately to whichever new address was on the back. She wrote long letters, filled with spelling errors and childish penmanship. Sometimes, if there was nothing happening to write about, she made up lies. Over each lower case 'i' she drew a tiny heart where the dot should be.

In school, she had struggled. The boys were overwhelmed by her looks and the racing curves of her body, and they treated her badly for it, as though her existence was a challenge and insult to their not-yet-manhood. The girls, in their jealousy, treated her just as badly, and so over the years she turned in on herself. After she stopped attending school, there were rumors about Marlene that came spilling out in laughter. One rumor had her turning tricks in Boston. One had her dead of an overdose. Even the teachers and staff shared the ever-changing reports. The rumors changed weekly, but Marlene was gone then and so she never heard them.

Five nights a week, she stripped at the Cat Club, a suburban strip bar thirty miles south along the highway near the Massachusetts border. The area was seedy, dirty, and most of the businesses were said to be mob owned. The first night she stripped, she had bummed a ride from a friend of her brother's, shown a fake I.D. to enter and won the amateur night contest. The manager asked her a few questions and within twenty minutes she had secured a regular slot at the club – Wednesday through Sunday. After a week, Marlene had saved enough to buy a used car with cash from one of the many lots in the surrounding towns. She bought a Cabriolet with 100,000 miles – the odometer lied. Her older brother's friend, persuaded by her flirtations, helped her forge signatures and arrange for the plates and registration, and she lost her virginity to him in the cramped back seat of the Cabriolet. The event was quick, not entirely unpleasant, and Marlene felt that at least it was over with.

And so it was that Marlene Black had found her freedom and her new life at sixteen years of age. She got along well with the other dancers and for the first time in her life she found herself among people for whom her physical self wasn't a problem. The bouncers and DJs at the club watched over her and while they lusted for her as well, they treated her in some ways like a kid sister. One of them always walked her to her Cabriolet at the end of the night, making sure there was no trouble with customers. Marlene started seeing one of the bartenders occasionally, though it wasn't serious.

The men who ran the strip club were rough, but they were businessmen and they knew Marlene brought business. The club was owned by a sixty-year-old Italian named Dominic Da Vota. Dominic only came to the club twice a month, usually during the afternoon, to reconcile the books, cut checks and pay bills. In spite of his age he was a powerful man: big, strong, and the air seemed to change in his presence. Everyone knew when Dominic was in the building. The beer-swilling patrons in their work shirts, their names patched onto their shoulders, and the scotch-drinking businessmen who should have been sitting in hotel conference rooms could feel the weather change when Dominic Da Vota entered the building. Dominic never watched the girls. He did his business then he left, leaving everyone tight as a devil's knot in his wake.

One April afternoon, Da Vota arrived at the club as usual to work out the accounts. A hard, cold rain blasted outside and so there were not many patrons in the club. The girls were going though the motions but without much motivation from the few men inside. Dominic worked out the accounts, cut a few checks, and handed them around. Unusually for him, he then went behind the bar, poured a tall whiskey and sat himself down at one of the small round tables. He stared out the window at the lashing rain. One of the bouncers approached him nervously.

"I can get you an umbrella."

"Nah, I'll just wait it out a bit."

"I can go pull your car round to the back door if you want."

"Do I look like Elizabeth Taylor to you?"

"Sorry, Mr. Da Vota, I was just trying to help if you wanted to leave."

"You want me to leave?"

"No, no, it's just you don't usually stay is all."

"I'm gonna have a drink in my own place if that's okay with you."

"Of course. If you want me to order food for you, let me know."

"Have you ever seen me eat in this fuckin' place?"

"No. I'm just trying to get you what you want."

"I want you to stop asking me what I want. If I want something from you you'll know it."

Dominic rolled his eyes and took a long swallow of his expensive whiskey, then leaned back in his chair, looked outside at the rain again, and heaved a huge sigh. Da Vota sat for a long time. The tension in the room was thick with him there. A few hours passed by and he filled his tall whiskey several times. At 7 PM, Marlene took her first shift of the evening to the sound of "Highway to Hell." The small crowd of men moved closer to the stage. Dominic gestured to the bouncer.

"Who is that?"

"That's Marlene Black. Rick hired her a few months back."

"Jesus."

"Yeah, she's doing well. Makes buck. A lot of guys come back just for her."

"I can see why. She looks a little young. Did Rick check everything?"

"I don't know. He handles all that stuff."

"She looks a little young to me."

"You want me to get Rick?"

"No. I'll talk to him in a bit."

The bouncer went back to his station. Dominic sat and watched as Marlene went through her act – twenty minutes – five songs. When she finished the stage floor was littered with bills. Dominic got up from his table and went to the back office where he found the manager, Rick.

"That girl just now. She looks a little young."

"She's good, Dom, I checked all the boxes when we hired her."

"You sure? If she's under, it's my ass and you know what that means for your ass."

"I'm sure, she had I.D., she drives, she's making buck. She's making us buck."

"As long as you're sure…"

Dominic opened the back door to see about the rain, saw that it had slowed and left the building, walked around to the parking area, and got into his Cadillac. He turned the engine over but sat thinking for a few moments, oblivious to the sports radio station barking loudly about the Bruins' playoff chances. He couldn't get the picture of Marlene from his mind.

Marlene was finished for the night and sat backstage rubbing her feet. The other dancers were packing up their bags and waiting for the parking lot to clear of drunk customers so that they could be walked to their cars without bother.

"Did you see Dom in here earlier?" someone asked Marlene.

"Who is Dom?" asked Marlene

"He owns this place. And the restaurant across the street and a Cadillac dealership and the Main Street Diner in Saugus too."

"Whoa…really?" said Marlene, impressed. "What's he like?"

"He's Italian. This is the north end. What do you think he's like?"

"I don't know – that's why I'm asking."

"Three letters. M O B."

"No shit?"

"No shit. He's okay though. He's nice enough. He's just not somebody you want to mess with, you know? I just steer clear of him."

"I don't want to mess with him. I'm just curious. I thought Rick owned this place."

"Rick's just the manager. What the fuck? How long you been here?"

"A couple months."

"Rick just manages the place, but Dominic owns it. He's really fuckin' rich."

"Sounds like it."

Marlene put her boots and parka on, stuffed her g-string and outfits into her bag, and went to stand by the door. She was smoking a cigarette when one of the bouncers noticed her and came to walk her to her car.

"You shouldn't smoke. It's bad for you," he said.

"Lots of things are bad for me. I like bad things."

"Don't get to liking too many of 'em, too much. They'll take you down quicker than you think."

"Aww…so sweet. You're worried about me."

"Nah, I don't worry 'bout nothing. I work for Dominic Da Vota. I ain't got no worries and nothing to worry about. Except Dom." He laughed.

"He's that bad, huh?"

"No comment. I'm glad I work *for* him."

"I guess I do too, then."

"Yeah, I guess you do too."

Marlene unlocked her car door and got inside. She cracked the window and gave a tiny wave to the man.

When she arrived home she found her mother leaning against the counter, crying softly. Marlene made her way through the living room to her room. The living room was glowing in the dancing blue light of the television set. As she passed her father, he slurred in her direction.

"Wha you bin?"

"You won't remember even if I do tell you. Leave mom alone."

"I'd like ta leave her lone."

"She already is."

She opened her bedroom door, walked in and slid the bolt over. She undressed and counted her money into neat piles; straightening out the wrinkled bills that some men rolled up into balls to throw onstage, making it harder to gather up at the end of her routine. One of the other dancers had told her they did this to be degrading, to make you feel cheap as you gathered up the money. It didn't bother

Marlene. She had their damn money and a lot of it. Marlene counted out almost eight hundred dollars on the hardwood floor of her room. She folded the wad then stuffed the money under her mattress. She undressed, put on pink pajamas and got into bed. Her sleep was restless. She had strange dreams and thoughts of Dominic Da Vota, the mobster, crept at the edges of her sleep.

In his enormous and garish bed, Dominic Da Vota could not stop thinking about the girl. He wasn't sure what it was exactly. It worried him that she looked too young to be dancing. He knew that the club was watched. He had been shut down in the past after being set up by state liquor commission agents for serving to under-aged gophers. There was something about the girl that unsettled him. He couldn't put his thick finger on it. Eventually he found his way to a short and fretful sleep.

The next night at the club, Marlene prepared herself backstage for her routine. She put on long papery black gloves that went up past her elbows, a tiara, a black g-string and impossibly high heels. She sat waiting while another dancer finished her routine to an old hip-hop song. When "Highway to Hell" started and her stage name, Misty, was announced over the booming PA system, she took the stage and started. Cheers went up and men moved forward to the stage. As she went through her act she noticed that at the very back of the room Dominic DaVota was seated alone, a tall glass on the table in front of him. She went through her routine, gathered up the piles of bills that littered the stage, then went backstage again where she found Dominic waiting for her.

"They really like you," he said.

"They like naked."

"I've had this place for twenty years. They like naked you a lot."

"I don't like them back, but I like their pocket money."

"That's the only way to think about it."

"It's the only way I do."

"Where do you live?"

"Up in Portsmouth."

"So you're a little out of your element down here."

"I guess, but it's been working."

Dominic did not look her up and down when he spoke. He looked directly in her eyes though she was completely naked.

Out in the club there was a small hubbub about some I.D.s at the door, but the four young men were let in and as other young men left, they took one of the cramped small tables at the edge of the stage. The next dancer started her act. Marlene looked at the clock. She had forty minutes until her next routine as the club had only three dancers on Wednesdays. The men tended to stay for a shorter time earlier in the week. On Fridays and Saturdays, there were five dancers as the men tended to stay much longer and spend much more.

"You know who I am?"

"Yeah, you're Dominic. I was told to stay away from you."

Another dancer shot a subtle sideways glance at Marlene.

"I'm the one person in this place you don't need to worry about."

"Then I won't worry about you."

Dominic stuck out his big hand and shook Marlene's own small elegant hand, her thin fingers dwarfed gently in his.

"It's nice to meet you," he said, then walked away.

Marlene puttered backstage glancing at the clock to keep track of time. When her second spot came she took the stage again as Misty, to the same cheers.

At the front of the stage, she saw four vaguely familiar faces, and her heart raced.

"Hey, Marlene!" one of them yelled above the music.

She continued her routine but found herself fumbling.

"Hey, Marlene! Nice job you found yourself!" he yelled.

"Fuck off…" she said under her breath and continued.

One of the men stood up and held out a single dollar bill. She made her usual circle around the front of the stage taking the bills from the men, dancing for a short moment in front of each of them. She danced slightly longer for a five and longer still for a ten, but stopped before she got to the table of familiar faces and circled back the other way.

"Aw c'mon!" the young man said, waving the single dollar bill. "You know you want it!"

Marlene continued dancing and her heart continued to hammer in her chest. Each time she circled the front of the stage, she stopped before reaching the table that was ringed by older brothers of her former schoolmates.

"My money's not good enough for you?" he yelled.

Then the man fidgeted a twenty-dollar bill from his wallet. He held it out, waving it dramatically, a sloshing plastic cup of beer in his other hand. Marlene noticed the twenty. As her third song played, she rolled off the long gloves, slipped from her g-string, and circled the front again. Wild cheers went up and several men held out ten-dollar bills, which she took with a forced smile as she showed them what they'd paid for. From the corner of her eye she saw the twenty-dollar bill again. She could see that the four familiar men were drunk. This time she made her way all the way around to their table. She looked back at the DJ booth, trying not to catch the eyes of the drunk waving the twenty, and reached out for it. He pulled it back and Marlene felt it slide through her delicate fingers. Then he waved it again just out of her reach.

"That's all I get for a twenty?!" he yelled.

Marlene reached for the bill again but he held it too far back. She stumbled in her heels and tripped slightly before catching herself on the low brass railing that surrounded the stage. The four drunk men erupted in laughter. Still he waved the twenty at Marlene. She stood herself up, turned around at the very edge of the stage, spread her legs and bent over, then reaching between her legs, grabbed the bill hard from his hand. The man held onto the bill and it ripped in two as she pulled it. Marlene spun around.

"Fuck you!" she yelled.

"No thanks, I don't like sloppy seconds. You owe me twenty bucks, bitch!" the man yelled back, then threw his plastic cup of beer at her. Marlene kicked off her heels and ran backstage without them, tears filling her eyes.

Dominic DaVota's big right fist smashed into the man's mouth from the side and the man crumpled to the stinking carpet. One of the man's teeth was knocked back into his mouth like a fallen tombstone. Blood trickled from his jaw. His eyes were open, but vacant. Dominic grabbed the back of the man's shirt and dragged him through the room, his head banging into chairs and the hard edges of the tables as they went. The other three young men sobered as they watched. Their elbows were grabbed by the bouncers and they were roughly handled out through the front door. Outside, Dominic was standing over the bloodied young man as he lay on the wet pavement, trying to get his senses back.

"I'm looking right at your face, you piece of shit. I'm gonna remember it. If I ever see you near this place again, I'll stomp your fucking head 'til you're nothing but fucking juice. You fucking hear me? Look at me, you fuck." Dominic reached his thick arm back to swing again and one of the bouncers put his hand gently on Dominic's shoulder to stop him.

"Get rid of these fucking assholes," Dominic said more calmly, then walked back into the club.

The bouncers helped the young drunk man to stand then the other three young men cradled-walked him, shaking, to their car.

Backstage, Marlene sat in a metal folding chair, her face in her hands, sobbing.

"Jesus Christ. I've never seen Dom do that," said one of the dancers.

"No shit. That was crazy," said the other.

"You okay, honey?"

"I'm fine," said Marlene, through her tears.

The DJ announced the next dancer, and she went out onto the stage to a song by Poison. Cheers erupted. Back in his office, Dominic stared at his swollen hand. The man's tooth had left a deep gash at his knuckles. He went to the bathroom to wash the cut. The two middle-aged men at the urinals could not urinate until Dominic left.

"Jesus," said one quietly to the other.

"No, pretty sure that wasn't him," said the other.

Two weeks later, at home in the bathroom, the strip turned pale purple and a few days later the doctor confirmed Marlene was pregnant. She told nobody. It was very early and she wasn't showing. Marlene stopped seeing the bartender from the club, and after a few of his calls went unreturned, he left her alone.

One night, after her shift was over, Dominic Da Vota showed up at the club in his Cadillac. He went inside but did not go to his office, and instead waited by the exit quietly. The bouncers nodded hellos to him and he nodded back. The two bartenders looked at each other nervously. When Marlene came from the backstage dressing room, Dominic was still waiting near the exit.

"Hey, kid. Let me walk you to your car," he said

"I'll walk her, Dom," one of the bouncers said.

"No," said Dom.

Dominic held out his beefy arm and, not knowing what to do, Marlene put her arm in his.

"So what are you driving?"

"A Cabriolet."

"That one?" He pointed.

"Yup. I bought it the first week I started."

"That's not a good car."

"It was what I could afford. I paid cash."

Dominic walked her to the car. Marlene unlocked the door and popped inside, then rolled down the window. She did not light a cigarette.

"I'm sorry about the other night."

"It happens. Not very often, but it happens. Some people need reminding there are rules. You make some cake tonight, sweetheart?"

"Yeah, I did pretty good. Why did you drive out here?"

"I couldn't sleep. Been having trouble sleeping."

"Conscience?"

"I don't have one, kid."

"Must be nice."

"It works for me."

"Well, thanks for walkin' me."

"This is not a good car for you."

"Why?"

"It's just not. These little cars? They're no good."

Dominic stood in the parking lot and watched her turn north onto the highway then went to his Cadillac, drove home, and poured an enormous glass of whiskey.

Marlene continued dancing at the club and banking her money. Every morning when she woke, she weighed herself on the bathroom scale, then turned sideways in the mirror to see if her belly had begun to grow. Only the very smallest change had begun to show but something was at work in her mind and she could feel it churning.

A few more weeks passed. Marlene danced. She counted her money. One morning when she looked at her sideways view in the mirror, she could finally see the small bump. She packed a small suitcase then drove to the bank, emptied and closed her bank account, and left with a cashier's check for sixty-four thousand dollars. That night when she arrived at the club, she found Rick in his office.

"I'm all done."

"What? You're killing it. You're making serious buck."

"I know, but I'm all done."

"Is it about those guys from a few weeks ago? Because I can assure you they won't be back here."

"No. I'm just done. Tonight's my last shift. I should probably give some notice but there are girls who want these shifts, so you're all covered."

"Nothing I can say to keep you? We can probably roll back your stage fee."

"Nope. All done."

Marlene finished her shift. AC/DC. Aerosmith. She packed up her bag and went to wait by the door for someone to walk her to her car, but saw Dominic was again standing at the exit waiting for her. He thrust his big arm out and she took it and they walked out.

"I hear you're all done."

"Yeah. I told Rick when I got here today."

"You're making buck, kid. You sure?"

"I'm sure."

"Well, I figured you were sure anyway. I got something for you. You can call it a retirement gift."

"What do you mean?"

"Give me your keys."

"What?"

"Just give me your keys."

Dominic fumbled through the key ring, located the Cabriolet key, slid it off the ring, and slid another key onto the ring.

"I don't understand."

"That car you're driving is no good. Trust me. It's no good. This is your car now."

"Where? I don't understand."

Dominic pointed to a shining maroon Cadillac.

"That one. It's a six cylinder, so the gas mileage is decent. It's not new but it looks new. Only about twelve thousand miles on it. It's yours."

"How can you do that? I don't understand."

"Don't worry about it. I know the dealer. I got a really good bargain on it."

"I don't know what to say, Dom."

"You're retired now. You don't have to say anything. You don't work for me anymore."

Marlene opened the door and sat inside.

"It's a good color for a girl, right?"

"Dom, it's beautiful, but I'm still confused."

"Nothing to be confused about. That other car is a piece of shit. It's not safe. This is a good car. Solid."

Marlene got out of the car, leaned up and kissed Dominic softly on the cheek, then got back in the car. When she left the parking lot she drove south.

"Good," Dominic said under his breath.

Back at his house, Dominic DaVota sat in his palatial gaudy living room on his palatial gaudy sofa, a photograph of his dead daughter in his shaking hand. A deep red scar ran across his enormous knuckles. He wept quietly until he fell asleep.

Author Bio

Rod Picott is a former construction worker turned singer-songwriter. Born in New Hampshire and raised in South Berwick, Maine he has released nine albums since his debut *Tiger Tom Dixon's Blues* in 2000. Picott has lived in Nashville, Tennessee since 1994.

His poetry debut, *God in His Slippers*, was published by Mezcalita Press in 2017. Bestselling author Nicholson Baker praised the collection as "Life-loving poems that tell you what you need to know." *Out Past the Wires* is Rod Picott's first work of fiction.

For more information on his work, tour dates, music and future writing please visit: **www.rodpicott.com**

MEZCALITA
PRESS

An independent publishing company dedicated to
bringing the printed poetry, fiction, and non-fiction
of musicians who want to add to the power and
reach of their important voices.

CPSIA information can be obtained
at www.ICGtesting.com
Printed in the USA
LVHW01s0228151117
556320LV00001B/2/P